RED LETTER SLAY

A MAIL CARRIER COZY MYSTERY BOOK 8

TONYA KAPPES

D1522769

PREVIEW

Melissa looked at her watch. Her brows pinched as she let out a grunting noise like she was about to say something but didn't. She simply took the box and started to do what I'd asked.

When I got to the front, "What do you want?" I asked Iris.

She put the palm of her hand over the microphone and put it down to her side.

"I think there's going to be a storm." Her tired, middle-aged eyes looked at me as if she were in a trance.

"According to Horace's weather report, the day of the wedding is going to be iffy, but I think it's clear this week until then." I wondered why on earth Iris was trying to give me the weather.

"Not that kind of storm." She blinked a few times before her eyes really snapped into focus. "There's going to be a murder."

GET FREE BOOKS

Join Tonya's newsletter.
See all of Tonya's books.
Find all these links on Tonya's website, Tonyakappes.com.

Chapter 1

"One step. One." I held my finger up and jabbed it to the ceiling of the Sugar Creek Gap Rehabilitation Center. "Just one."

Vince Caldwell sat on the edge of the rehab center's white medical bed, his scrawny, age-spotted legs sticking out of the bottom of the blue gown. The slipper, which had seen much better days, dangled from his toes and hung low from his heels.

"One. Or how else will you get back home to the people who love you?" I questioned him. An unfortunate event that had made him take a nasty fall left him with a letter opener, of all things, jabbed into his brain.

"Fine." He gave in with a sigh.

The two nursing assistants stepped up to either side of Vince. Each one slipped their arm underneath his armpit and helped him to his feet. Once his feet landed on the old, yellowing twelve-inch tile floor, the three of them stood there for a few seconds.

"Do you have your footing, Mr. Caldwell?" the young man in the indigo scrubs asked while the other awaited Vince's reply. They noticed his nod. "Okay, now we are just going to stay on either side of you. All we need from you today is a couple steps, just like you're doing in physical therapy."

Vince looked at me from under his thick eyebrows. He gave a hard stare to the space in front of him, the empty space just waiting for him to step into it.

"I can't." He shook his head before leaning his body back as though he was about to sit down.

"Stop right there." I put my hand up, indicating for him to stop and for the assistants not to listen to him. "You've been in here for two months now. I'm not sure why you insist you aren't ready. You've been ready, and the doctor cleared you for today. That's why I'm here. Now"—I pointed at his feet—"let's take those steps just like you did in therapy yesterday."

I tried to encourage him without getting a wee bit irritated. I'd never seen Vince this way. Timid and almost old. Not that he was a spring chicken. He wasn't. He lived in the residential area of the Sugar Creek Gap Nursing Home in one of the independent condos next to my own parents.

I'd gotten to know the retired FBI agent as his mail carrier. Over the years, we'd become pretty close and even thought of ourselves as sleuthing buddies on a couple of different crimes in and around Sugar Creek Gap, so when I'd gotten a call from Vivian Tillett, the director of the nursing home, telling me Vince was dead, I was upset.

Vince was like an uncle to me.

And I sure was treating him as such with my forceful tone.

"I'm here to pick you up, and that means you've got to walk over to that bathroom and get your clothes on so I can take you home." I swung my finger and twisted my body, pointing at the bathroom door. "Get."

"You sound like you should be my kin instead of my mail carrier." Vince shook his head. He had no issues taking the first step and then the second and third. He ended up doing just fine.

The door from the hall swung open. Dr. Klonik rushed in, rubbing her hands together. She had her shoulder-length brown hair pulled back into a headscarf. Her five-foot, four-inch frame was small, but her personality was massive.

"Where's Vince?" She glanced at the empty room. "I figured he'd be standing at the door, waiting for me to sign off on those discharge papers after all this time."

"I think he's a little leery. Something about falling again." One of the assistants told Dr. Klonik something I never would've thought would describe how Vince felt. "He is acting like he's unable to walk this morning."

"I see." Her chin lifted, her eyes sliding toward me. "I think we can fix that."

About that time, Vince opened the bathroom door with his pajama pants still on, his robe open, the tie dangling down and brushing the sides of his knees. He shuffled across the tile, slippers swishing.

"Oh, Doctor. I didn't see you there." There was a hint of surprise on his face, though he'd tried to cover it up with a stoic hard jaw.

"I hear you're not wanting to really pick up those feet and walk." Her brows lifted, eyes looking at his legs. "Seems to me you can't walk. Which means I'll just send you home in a wheelchair. I'll have my assistant tell Vita you need to go over to the assisted living part for a few weeks. They'll need to keep an eye on you."

Vince got to high-stepping, a sudden shift in his physical state.

"Looks like the bathroom trip made me feel better. I don't need a wheelchair, and I certainly don't need to move out of my condo." He did an about-face and headed back into the bathroom. He muttered, "I'll be right back with my clothes on."

We waited until the door was shut before we all smiled.

"I guess you got him on that one." I walked over to the room's built-in cabinet, opened the double doors, and took out Vince's duffle bag, which I'd thrown a few things into after they'd discharged him from the hospital to the rehabilitation center.

"A man of Vince's stature has a big ego that plays into things. No one wants to move into assisted living if they don't have to." The assistant stuck a piece of paper in front of Dr. Klonik, and she signed it. "I have already talked to his children. They will be traveling in to see him this weekend. They said it was fine he was released in your care." She handed me the piece of paper to sign.

"That's great." I scribbled my signature.

I'd been in constant contact with his family since the day he'd been taken to the hospital, and his daughter Mandie had been worried sick. I'd stayed at the hospital until Mandie had gotten to town. Of course, I'd told her to take her time. Vince was critical, but luckily he'd been taken back into surgery, where the trauma doctors had worked their magic.

Vince came out in much more appropriate clothing.

"All ready?" I asked him.

"It's as good a time as any," he said with a quiver in his voice. He sat down in the wheelchair for his export out of this joint.

"All righty now, Vince." Dr. Klonik handed him some discharge papers. "I'll see you back in my office for a follow-up next week." The assistant pushed Vince out the door and down the hall.

Dr. Klonik and I followed behind.

"The day and time are written right there on the page." She pointed at the paper jiggling in his hand from the bumpy ride.

The date and time were highlighted in pink. She gazed my way.

Our eyes caught. Chalk it up to women's intuition. I knew she was letting me know to make sure it got on Vince's busy social calendar, which was currently wide open—at least enough for him to get to his appointment. Now I couldn't guarantee the ladies who lived in the facility wouldn't fall over one another to get to him. Without fail, one of them would be waiting patiently for me when I delivered the mail to see if she could get some insider information about Vince's arrival time. By the sounds of it, they all planned to make him some casseroles to come home to.

"It's not on bingo day, is it?" Vince's question caught my ear.

The assistant stopped at the big circular revolving door that was large enough to push his wheelchair around and outside.

"If it is, you're going to miss it." She patted him on the back as he folded the paper to slip it in the pocket of his denim button-down shirt. "You call me if you have any problems, but you're doing good. You're a strong man, Vince Caldwell. You really are lucky the letter opener didn't cause any brain damage."

"Thank you, Doctor." Vince grabbed his duffle bag from me. "Let's go, Bernie."

"Wow, you sure did get a hop in your step." It took me a couple of skips to get up to him.

"Well, I guess right now is a better time than any," he muttered, picking up his feet for me to push him on out to my truck.

I opened the door, and before I got to him, he was up on his feet.

"What was all that hemming and hawing around about not walking?" I knew Vince Caldwell, and he had something up his sleeve.

"I've been in there doing a lot of thinking." He reached up, grabbed the handle on the inside of the truck, and hoisted himself in. "You know, there's not much to do in a place like that but think. Even when I was in the hospital laid up on that ventilator. Those beeping machines going off every five minutes 'cause I moved my arm one way and turned it another. The nurses talking in the hall. They tell you rest is the best thing for your body, but that place don't let you rest."

He stopped talking long enough for me to sit in the driver's seat and get my seat belt on before he continued.

"You check that date. I'm not missing bingo night." He really surprised me.

On the rare occasions he came to bingo, it was often only because I would beg him to help Iris Peabody, my best friend—and to help me too. There was just something fishy about bingo being on his mind.

Luckily, I didn't have to ask to find out. He told me.

"Do you honestly think I slipped, fell, and landed on a letter opener when I don't even own a letter opener?" The dark circles under his eyes told me just how much his mind had been rolling since he'd been here and how little sleep he'd had. "Have you ever seen me open any mail you deliver with a letter opener?"

I took a second to think about it. Using the ponytail holder around my wrist, I pulled back my long auburn hair so it was out of my way while I got him situated back into his normal life.

"No. I've only seen you rip things open or in half when you didn't want to open them." In fact, I didn't remember ever seeing a letter opener in his condo at the facility either.

His brows lifted. "Told ya."

Vince took pride in his age and appearance. He was always up earlier than anyone else in the senior living facility, and he had already exercised, taken a shower, and gotten dressed for the day. This was early, since the facility was the first stop on my deliveries. I'd never seen circles under Vince's eyes.

Ever.

"I don't know. Did someone come in to visit and just so happen to have a letter opener?" I asked, pushing the truck key into the ignition, turning the engine over.

"Someone came to visit, all right." Vince's tone was far from the quiver I'd heard a few minutes ago. "Someone came to kill me. You and I are going to find out."

Chapter 2

"Tried to kill him?" Iris Peabody, my best friend, dug her fists into the new gluten-free pie dough she was trying out for the first time.

She picked up the ball, tossing between her hands a couple of times before the disgust leveled on her face. Frustrated, she used the back of her hand to brush back the small strands of brown hair that had found their freedom from underneath the hairnet. She tossed it back into the bowl and threw a sprinkle of something on top of the doughy ball before she started to knead it again.

"Yep. So he insisted he's going to bingo tonight." I knew I had to get going if I was going to join Iris there. She'd been volunteering her time to call bingo for the senior living facility for too many years to count.

"You better get him there early." She picked up the dough. A smile crossed her face. She set it back in the bowl, picked up the ink pen on the workstation, and jotted something down.

As the owner of Pie in the Face Bakery, Iris took her work very seriously while she was creating something new. This was not just any something new. It was a very special pie she was making.

My granddaughter Clara Butler's birthday pie. Plus, it was a trial run for Iris to make gluten-free pies for my wedding reception, which was coming up. Actually, my wedding was in just a few days, and I'd made sure the post office had scheduled me to work up until the day before so I could keep my mind off of the event.

Not that I didn't want to marry Mac Tabor. I most certainly was ready to tie the knot, but I had to make sure Vince was able to come, since he was so special to me. Mac and I had tentatively planned the wedding around a few dates the doctor had given based on Vince's rehabilitation stay.

"Those women are going to be fighting over which table they think he's going to be sitting at." Iris grabbed one of the glass pie plates from one of the shelves in the bakery's kitchen area. She used her fingers to fit the dough perfectly along the inside, pinching the top edges perfectly. "If you tell them he was the target of someone trying to kill him, then they might not want to sit next to him," Iris said with a snicker.

"It's not funny. He really does think someone tried to kill him." Though I felt the same way Iris did, I didn't tell her so. "Which means I'll entertain what he has to say. Take a few notes. Keep an ear open while on my route, and..." I was stumped for an "and."

"And what? Not get married? Go on a honeymoon because Vince thinks you two should be playing Sherlock Holmes and Watson of Sugar Creek Gap?" Iris had gone over to the walk-in refrigerator and pulled out a bowl of apples she'd already prepared for the filling. "Clara is going to love her birthday pie."

"She sure is." Clara had been such a blessing to our family. Her first birthday was coming up, which was going to be an even bigger party than my own wedding. That was fine with me. "I really appreciate you making this gluten free."

"Whatever that sweet baby wants." Iris was playing nice. Both of us had talked about this whole no-gluten lifestyle Julia and Grady had adopted since Julia started trying to get pregnant again.

Grady, my son, went along with whatever Julia wanted and had been doing really well with the new lifestyle. But my parents—whoowee, they were a different story.

"Speaking of the sweet baby." I got up but not without grabbing one of the spoons off of the preparation table to get a scoop of the apple filling for a quick taste. "Mmmmm, mmmm."

"At least there's some good old-fashioned sugar in there." Iris winked and poured the rest of the bowl in the pie dish.

A stove timer buzzed. Iris left the pie and walked over to the stove. With oven mitts on, she reached into the oven and pulled out a tray bearing two pies. The filling of each had bubbled up through the slits in the golden crust.

Just looking at the pies made my mouth water.

"Don't worry. One of these is for you and Mac." Iris winked and left them on the cooling rack. "You can grab it after bingo. It'll make for a delicious night treat. A scoop of ice cream." Iris's shoulders rose to her ears in delight.

"You know me too well." I studied my friend, who I'd known since childhood.

There were so many dreams between us, and there was no better feeling than sitting in the kitchen she'd dreamed of for so long.

Not until her ex-husband had cheated on her did she truly go after her dream of owning her own bakery. Not the actual cheating part, the part in which he and his mistress had decided to eat some of Iris's homemade pie. It wasn't just that they ate it, though. It was what they ate it out of.

A pie plate.

Yep. To Iris, her pie plates were sacred, and no one ate out of a pie plate. That led to Iris catching them eating out of the pie plate, and she sorta went a little nuts. The pie was no longer in the pie plate but all over her ex and the mistress.

At least Richard, my dead husband, was good for one thing besides Grady. Richard did come up with the name Pie in the Face. He meant it as a joke, referring to Iris's ex. That was when she decided baking in my kitchen and hers was more than a hobby. She'd been making cakes and pies for people for hire already, but it was nothing like a business.

Her business was born out of a horrible situation. Those were the times I knew things we couldn't explain happened for a reason. Unfortunately, it could take years to realize just what the reason was.

I looked back at the pie Iris was making for Clara, thinking of how Grady and Julia weren't able to conceive another child. Yet.

"I've got to finish delivering the mail before bingo." I reached into the mailbag and got out the next stack of rubber band-bound mail. When I hoisted the mailbag up on my shoulder, I realized I'd not dropped off Leotta Goldey's mail.

Instead of even mentioning it to Iris, I wagged the mail in the air over my shoulder. "Keep your ear open for who might want to have killed Vince."

I loved our little town of Sugar Creek Gap, Kentucky. The town was small, but the hearts in it were big. The summer break had proved to be a great time to have the wedding. Mac and I were able to host it outside on my family's farm, where Grady and Julia lived in the farmhouse. It was a perfect place to raise Clara.

My parents raised me there, and I raised Grady there, and now Clara was going to carry on the tradition. I'd love to say that about Clara specifically, but Julia and Grady's determination to have another child told me I was going to have more than one grandbaby. That was fine with me. I had a lot of love to go around.

Social Knitwork was the first business I came to on the second loop of my deliveries, but today my mind was filled with Vince and what he'd told me.

"Bernadette Butler," Leotta said with a tsking sound when I walked into her yarn shop. "Might be the last time I say that." She tugged the reading glasses off her nose and winked. "When I noticed you walking on by with your head in the clouds a little bit ago, I knew you were all aflutter about your upcoming nuptials."

"I'm sorry. I took too long talking to Iris. She's busy making a pie for Clara's first birthday." I unbound the mail stack, thumbed through it just to find her mail, and exchanged it for a stack she needed to go out.

"Yes. I heard something about the pie Julia requested." Leotta wasn't one to keep her mouth shut. "Your mama sure isn't happy about it. She said she's made all of y'all's first birthday cakes. And I told your mama how this generation is just different."

Leotta leaned up against the counter, resting her hip as she took a big bite of buttermilk biscuit from a place I'd recognize anywhere—the Wallflower Diner. The diner my parents owned, which proudly served southern food and included a menu full of gluten.

"Anyways, she'll come around." Leotta brushed her hands off the apron she wore around the yarn shop. "I made you something special. You stay right there."

She disappeared into the next room, where she taught classes, and I couldn't help but look around while she ran in there to get what she had for me. Social Knitwork was a cute yarn shop with a couple of different rooms. The front room was a little shop where Leotta sold all the cute scarves, hats, and various items that could be monogrammed. The counter and checkout were also located there.

We southerners loved to wear our initials with pride. A lot of merchandise in the shop had the Sugar Creek High School Grizzly on it too. This place was my one-stop shop for all my game-day needs. Especially on football days, only because Grady was the football coach, and let's just say I was in the stands to root him on for each game.

"Here you go." Leotta reappeared, holding a brown bag with a bow attached to the front. "I want you to open it now."

"Are you sure?" I asked and dropped my bag to the floor.

"Of course I am. I made it especially for you." How could I not open the bag as pride spilled out of her?

It was nice getting gifts for the wedding, but Mac and I were in our fifties, and this wasn't my first go-around. It was Mac's, but still.

I took out the hooded shirt and held it up in front of me so I could see all of it.

The shirt displayed an embroidered emblem of the Grizzly mascot along with my initials, but where the *B* for Butler should've been, there was a *T* for Tabor, which would be my new last name.

"I wanted you to have something ready to go before the next big game." Leotta's brows pinched. "Will you even be in town for the game?"

"Of course." I held the shirt up to my chest so she could get a look. "Mac and I don't plan on going on a honeymoon just yet. I love it."

Leotta clapped her hands together.

"I'm so glad. You've got all the other initialed items with your old initials that I just hate for you to even wear them." Leotta was so kind. "Now you can wear that, and you can pick out anything else you want to put your new initials on."

"No. No." I folded the shirt back up and placed it in my

mail carrier bag. "I will buy more. I promise, but I have to get out of here so I can get to bingo on time."

"I heard Vince came home this morning." Leotta made her way back around to her biscuits. "What's this I hear about someone trying to kill him?"

"No one tried to kill him," I assured her. "If they did, don't you think Angela would've been all over it?"

"Do you think he's getting a little older?" Leotta didn't say it, but she was referring to his memory loss.

"No. I think he's going to be fine." I picked up the bag as we said our goodbyes.

The fall in Sugar Creek Gap happened to be my favorite season. The trees were still full of leaves, but that foliage had turned to the burnt oranges, yellows, and reds that made the hills of Kentucky so delightful to the eye.

Though the weather hadn't turned completely to the autumn temperatures that sat in the fifties, every once in a while I'd get a little chill as the breeze swept along the road, making the freshly fallen tree leaves dance.

The tickle of a light chill got me excited for not only snuggling up with my new husband but for my job. I loved being a mail carrier in our little town. Mail carriers knew so much about their clients. Not because we could see into what was really going on in their lives or how they did business, since we saw all the mail they got, but because we would stop and chat and check on one another. And everyone was doing that today.

"There you are." Mom had her eagle eye on the door of the diner, waiting for me to appear. "I've been waiting all morning for you. Did you hear about our baby Clara's birthday pie?"

Mom patted around her apron to dry off her hands before they found their way into her brown hair and repositioned the bobby pins.

"It's a disgrace to have a gluten-free pie for your first birthday." She threw her hands up in the air and turned around. She grabbed a Styrofoam box off the counter and set it next to the register, where her outgoing mail leaned against the stack of diner menus. "I told Grady they can't live on seeds and berries. My granddaughter isn't going to live on seeds and berries."

Tears welled up in her hollow eyes.

"I wished you'd talk some sense into your mom." Dad sat in his usual spot at the bar, letting her do more work than she should. He would pick up the slack after the morning breakfast crowd and his friends left.

Dad's buddies had been coming to the diner for as long as I could remember, and I remembered way back when they brought me here every day until I was old enough to go to school. Back then, kindergarten wasn't required, but I begged them to let me go so I didn't have to serve coffee at the ripe age of five.

"Mom." I handed Dad the bills they'd gotten in the mail. He curled his nose, pooh-poohing them to look at later.

I sat my mailbag down next to Dad and made my way around the counter. I gave Mom a little hug around her plump waist.

"We have to let Julia and Grady raise Clara. They know what they are doing." I might not understand or agree with them, but she was their daughter. "Besides, if they hear you keep talking about it all over town, they are going to get upset."

"I am upset. Highly." She stopped plunging her fists into her thick hips. "What are they going to do if they hear I'm upset? Not let her see me?"

"Well." I pinched my lips and shrugged, knowing well that could happen, though I thought Julia and Grady were a little more adult than my mother was being.

"They wouldn't dare." Mom held her hands to her chest. "Would they?"

Her eyes darted back and forth between mine, looking for some sort of confirmation or denial.

"Oh my stars. I've not talked about it all over town." She started to backtrack. "I guess Iris Peabody will be able to make a good gluten-free pie, and I could try to just use one cup of flour instead of three."

"No flour. They don't want Clara getting sick, and they want her immune health to be optimal. They said with all the antibiotics." I was going to launch into the big, long speech Grady had given me after I'd nearly lost my marbles when he told me about the gluten-free pie.

"Next thing I know, you're going to tell me you're having a gluten-free menu for the wedding." She stopped and looked at me. "Oh my Lordy." She took the towel from over her shoulder and flung it on the ground.

"I have to make sure everything is organic." I prepared myself for a tongue-lashing. "Antibiotics and pesticides..." I started to go down the whole speech Grady had given me.

"Antibiotics, whatever." Dad threw in his two cents. "We're all gonna die of something. Me personally, I'd love to die by the way of your mom's cooking."

"Me too." I decided to just keep quiet. It was best to stay neutral. "Who's this for?" I asked and opened the container.

"Vince Caldwell. I heard he came home, and he likes my homemade sausage gravy with flour." She emphasized the word "flour."

"I already saw him. Can't Dad take it over to him?" I asked.

"No. Your father needs to stay here and take care of the diner. I've gotten a sudden headache, and I need to go upstairs to lie down for a minute." Mom untied her apron. "I can't believe you are on their side." She stormed off from the diner and into the hall, where a flight of stairs led to a top-floor apartment they'd recently renovated to use as an Airbnb.

Apparently, it was vacant, and Mom had taken to the bed over the gluten thing.

"Don't you worry about her." Dad picked up the bag and handed it to me before he gave me a hug. "She'll be all right. When you were a baby, and the doctor told her not to give you fresh cow's milk, she almost took his head off with her swinging pocketbook. Look at you now. You turned out fine as frog hair."

"Thanks, Dad." I hoisted the bag on my shoulder.

"You have enough on your plate to worry about. How are you doing? Ready to walk down that aisle again?" He smiled.

I could still clearly remember the day he walked me down the aisle so I could marry Grady's father. He actually asked me if I really wanted to marry Richard Butler, and I said of course I did. He was what I'd thought was the love of my life. We were married when he had his fatal car wreck, and Grady was in high school. Years later, I'd found out Richard had been living a double life, but it was all under the bridge.

Today I was confident that I wanted to spend the rest of my life with Mac Tabor. What was left of my life, anyway.

"Have you two thought about where you're going to live?" Dad asked.

"I imagine on Little Creek Road, where we live now." My answer had a bit of a sarcastic bite because of a sore spot Mac and I were having about who would move in with who.

"I know he's an architect, but is it legal to build a tunnel or a bridge over the houses between yours?" Dad joked.

"I guess it's not important right now. We just want to get married, get on with our lives, and enjoy Clara along with the rest of our family." Over the customers' chatter in the diner, the sprayer from the kitchen, and the sizzle of the gridiron in the back, I could hear Lucy Drake giving the morning's report on the radio from the speakers. "I'm late."

I kissed my dad on the forehead, grabbed Vince's

container, and headed out the door. Luckily, the next few stops between the diner and the radio station were in and out. No major chitchat, and since Tabor Construction was Mac's, I could hand him his mail tonight.

On any given day, I would be fine with being a little behind, which wasn't unusual, since my customers loved to talk to me and catch up on things. But there was still so much to do for the wedding, and now that Vince believed his fall was an attempt on his life—well, I found myself wondering just who it could've been.

Lucy was the morning DJ of the WSCG radio station, which was just on the corner of Main Street and Short Street, where I'd finish up my second loop of deliveries.

On a good day, I'd always deliver the station's mail before Lucy hit the airwaves. On a late day, I made it to the station just as she was putting on her big earphones, not sending the weather broadcast over to Horace LeLand, the new weatherman.

Leave it to Lucy to be too much of a diva to continue reading the bulletin from the weather department, which was literally all she ever did.

The DJ booth was behind two walls of glass. No matter the time of day, you could stand out on the sidewalk on Main Street or Short Street and watch the DJ. The big red sign inside above the DJs' heads flashed On Air.

"Don't worry, folks. The weather will have turned just in time for you to get out those big quilt blankets, hand warmers, and ear mitts for the big game between the Grizzlies and the Musketeers. We are expecting the temperature to drop down into the mid-fifties by the end of the week, so if you have any outdoor events, like a wedding…" Horace slid his gaze to me when he saw me walk up. Obviously, he was talking to me. "I'd suggest you order some heat lamps because it'll dip down into the cool forties before midnight. Go Grizzlies!"

"How do you think the Grizzlies are looking this year, Horace?" Lucy Drake was also at the microphone. She leaned on the desk with her left forearm as she shifted her face to look at him.

"I think Mac Tabor has done wonders since Coach Butler put him on staff. Mac isn't from Sugar Creek Gap, like me, but he brings big moves and plays like me." I watched as Horace smiled, wiggling his brows at the lady standing behind Lucy.

Someone I didn't know. The radio station funneled so many people in and out that it was hard to keep track of them all. Horace and Melissa LeLand had come to Sugar Creek Gap over the summer. Though I knew very little about them, my mom raved about how much she liked Melissa's mom, Sandra Rothchester, who lived in the retirement community with them and Vince.

I wouldn't think anything of the woman with short red hair, who was thin, wore a maxi dress, and held a clipboard to her chest, but she was blushing. She was almost gushing from Horace giving her the slightest attention—and, well, for the fact he was married.

But to each his own, I thought as I slipped the mail into the mail slot, preparing myself for Little Creek Road, where I knew the Front Porch Ladies would greet me.

Chapter 3

"He said someone tried to kill him." I saw my duck friend waiting for me, paddling away underneath the bridge as I crossed over Little Creek on Short Street. "Who on earth would stab someone with a letter opener? In their head?"

My little daily rendezvous with the duck was something I looked forward to. One day, I hoped to introduce Clara to him, since I lived on Little Creek Road, where the Little Creek ran along. Across the street from my house, another bridge crossed the creek, forming a shortcut back to Main Street. The duck met me there, too, so it would be easy to make the introduction once Clara got bigger.

I liked to think the duck loved my company instead of the bag of duck feed I kept in the mailbag.

"Why am I even thinking about this when I have my wedding coming up? I need to be thinking about that." I sighed. "I'll see you at the end of the street," I called as I threw in one last handful of feed down to him.

Little Creek Road was just a short street with a few houses on the right side only. Mac's house was first. That arrangement gave me the argument that it was located on the corner of two roads and therefore very dangerous to Clara, whereas my house was at the very end of the dead-end street and thus very safe for Clara. In between were the Front Porch ladies, whose diligent eyes made the entire street safe.

Harriette Pearl, Ruby Dean, Gertrude Stone, and Millie Barns had their fingers on the pulse, and that meant Vince Caldwell.

"How did he look?" Harriette asked. "I heard he had a gaping hole right here." She pointed at her temple, her grey brows knotted.

"I heard it was the other side," Gertrude mentioned.

"It had to be on the outside if they stabbed him." Ruby Dean shook her head.

"I said other side," Gertrude said, voice raised so Ruby could hear her. "Turn up your ears!" She used her hand to motion.

"Who said anything about stabbing?" I asked the ladies as I handed each of them her own stack of mail.

They'd been waiting for me on Harriette's front porch, no doubt because it was the first of their houses and next to Mac's.

"Your mom told us not to tell you." It was Gertrude's way of letting me know. "And you know that boy of yours is about to put her into an early grave with all this business about cooking with no flour. Who on earth ever heard of such?"

"It is a thing." Revonda Gail Stone, Gertrude's daughter, was also on the porch. She lived right next door to me. "They've even started putting little G's next to items on menus in some restaurants in Lexington. I didn't know what it meant, and the waitress told me it was a thing now."

"There are legitimate reasons people don't eat gluten." I was finding myself educating them, since I had had to go to the Sugar Creek High School for a booster meeting in the school's library and took the opportunity to look it up after the meeting. "Celiac disease, for one."

When I found myself rattling off a few statistics about migraines and various other things, I could see the ladies' eyes glazing over.

"Enough talk about food." Revonda Gail tried to save me.

"Food? There's never enough talk about food." Harriette Pearl snickered. "But I know you want to stop talking about it, so we will. Let's get back to Vince. Do you think someone tried to kill him?"

"I don't think so, but he insists on it." I gnawed my lip, wondering if I should say it or not. I did. "Vince has never insisted on anything since I've known him, even when we did know a murder had been committed, and we'd snooped around. Then he'd say to consider all the possibilities."

"I wonder if he's just too close to the incident, and he can't even believe he'd fall, much less on a letter opener." Revonda Gail thumbed through her mail.

"Men have such high egos. Especially retired FBI agents." Gertrude ripped a couple of pieces of mail in half and made a little pile of mail trash next to her. "I'd just keep him happy until he gets settled at home a little more. Once they get home, men tend to forget all the crazy stuff they think up inside those hospital rooms."

"He's been in therapy, Mom," Revonda Gail reminded Gertrude.

"I know that." Gertrude's face squished. "Do they give medicine? Do they have doctors come see you in there?"

Revonda Gail nodded, smiling slightly.

"Then it's a hospital." Gertrude huffed, crossing her arms over her chest.

"Look who's being bullheaded now." Revonda Gail got up to leave.

"I'll walk with you. I've got to get my third loop delivered. Ladies, I'll see you later today," I told them.

"You didn't even tell us about any new wedding plans." Ruby was the one who always wanted all the details.

"Nothing to tell. Everything is still on this weekend at the farm until further notice." I waited for Revonda Gail at the bottom of the steps that led up to Harriette's porch while she hugged her mom goodbye.

"Did you hear Horace's weather report?" Harriette asked.

"Yeah, but I'm hoping he's wrong. The big game looks like it's going to be fine." Everyone was excited in anticipation of our first preseason home football game on Friday night.

Mac and I had decided not to have any sort of rehearsal dinner—or any rehearsal at all. We'd rather just stand up in front of our friends and family and say "I do," and there was no rehearsal for that. There was no way Mac would miss the game now that he was on coaching staff and not just volunteering to help Grady.

"I hope you're not listening to them." Revonda Gail's hair was wadded up in a banana clip in the back of her head. She had her typical short shorts on but this time wore a sweatshirt too.

"They don't bother me." She and I walked down the street and briefly stopped for a minute before her front gate. "How's the new gig?"

Revonda Gail had been selling CBD products out of her home. She'd still not told anyone but me about it. I had to believe someone suspected something. The FedEx man was there more than Revonda Gail was, and with the Front Porch Ladies always on the lookout, I knew one of them had to have been counting just how many times the delivery truck zoomed up and down Little Creek Road on any given day.

I wasn't sure who she worked for or if she worked for

herself. The only thing I did know was her rent check was always in my mailbox the first of the month waiting for Mac.

"It's good. Another thing the nosy broads have been craning their necks to see. Even followed the delivery truck down here one day when I was gone to the grocery store." Revonda Gail had gotten herself in trouble a time or two, and I was sure the Front Porch Ladies only wanted to make sure she had finally gotten on the straight and narrow road. "You're trying to get off the subject of something."

"What?" I laughed. "No. I just want to make sure you're good."

The loud woof from my house next door caught our attention. Buster, my chocolate lab, was looking out the house's front window, and Rowena, my orange tabby cat, was sitting on the windowsill. They both watched me like hawks.

"The kids are calling me, and I better go let them out before I have to get my third loop delivered. I'll talk to you later." There was no better time for my fur babies to have seen me.

The less I had to talk about all the things in my head, the better for everyone.

Chapter 4

The dining hall in the senior living facility was where all the activities took place. Bingo was especially popular because of one person.

Iris Peabody. Well, that was until today, now that Vince was back and had all the residents up in a tizzy about a killer.

Iris was very popular in the community. She would bring all sorts of desserts, and the residents of the Sugar Creek Gap Senior Living Facility loved all things sweet. And there was no limit to how many servings Iris let them have, unlike the dietician who stood over them during the dining hours.

Iris had them fooled. Everything she made was sugar-free, which meant no one was left out.

The Pie in the Face Bakery truck was pulled up to the front of the facility, the vehicle's two back doors wide open. Inside, two more boxes of goodies Iris had yet to get lay on a couple of the wire baking racks.

I grabbed the boxes, used my hip to shut the two doors, and I headed inside.

"You're late!" Iris yelled. She was at the long banquet table, laying out the desserts. "I'm doing your job."

"I know. My day." I put the two boxes down and gave her a hug. "I even drove the LLV for my last loop."

"I'm shocked." Iris's eyes grew big.

"I did want to walk it, but I knew I had to be here in time." The desserts were calling to me. "And no matter what I do"—I looked down and rubbed the gut I'd gotten since going through menopause—"this isn't going away until I cut all my carbs, eat lettuce, and do one thousand sit-ups every hour."

There were plenty of brownie bites on the table, so I grabbed one and peeled back the paper cover.

"I'm stressed." I popped the treat into my mouth.

"I'll have one for you too." Like a true friend, Iris grabbed one too. "Friends don't let friends menopause alone."

"Thank you." I nodded, sending us both into a fit of laughter.

"Seriously, the wedding?" she asked. She took one of the boxes I brought in. I put the desserts in my box, and she placed the desserts in the other box. We worked like the good team we were. "Clara's pie?"

"I wish it were those things. But it's Vince. I can't wait for you to see him. Talk to him. He is convinced someone tried to kill him." No matter what I'd tried today, I couldn't get his theory, no matter how silly it was, out of my head.

To continue getting ready for the game, Iris had gone over to the table in the very front. There, the bingo sphere with all the little Ping-Pong bingo balls would soon be spinning. The tables were still arranged like it was suppertime, so I had to take off the white linen tablecloths and replace them with the cute bingo-themed ones Iris had found online. She insisted they'd give the elderly more excitement than the normal white tablecloths.

She was right. The first time the cute, colorful bingo-ball-patterned tablecloths made their appearances, the residents went nuts.

Some of the residents were shut-ins and unable to leave. That was why we were here—to make this experience as special as possible. The chairs were also placed strategically. Even though no one liked to claim they had their spot, they did. Some chairs I knew had to be positioned closer than others because some of our elderly friends were harder of hearing than their fellows. These residents required a good friend to sit next to them to recite the numbers three or four more times than Iris did over the microphone.

It'd become our little ritual, and I was happy to do it, which brought me right back around to the knowledge that if someone was in the senior living facility trying to kill people, then I had to take it seriously.

"There you are," Vince called from the entrance of the dining hall. "I thought you were going to come get me so we could talk." He twisted his head to look around, apparently making sure we were alone. "We have to discuss this letter opener issue."

"I had to work." I pulled a chair out for him.

"It looks like you are getting around much better than this morning," he said.

I gave him the side-eye.

"The only reason I wasn't ready to come back was because I know someone tried to kill me, and I didn't have a plan. I have a plan now." Vince surprised me with his enthusiasm. "I think they had mistaken me for someone else."

"Why is that?" I wondered because everyone knew Vince.

"My unit was one of the condos getting new carpeting." He started his tale, and I noticed an older lady coming into the dining hall a little early but didn't pay her too much attention. "I told Vivian I was more than happy to stay in the assisted living part of the community so they didn't have to rush. No problem, right?"

"Right." I agreed but quickly realized I shouldn't've.

"Wrong." He pointed his crooked finger at me.

"Wrong?" My eyes narrowed in question.

"Right. You are wrong. That's when someone mistook me for someone else. They thought I was the person who normally stayed in the room, and that's when they tried to off me." He had come up with an elaborate scheme even I was having a hard time following.

"Then it should be easy to find out who stayed in there before you and Vivian is able to tell us." It seemed simple enough.

"Mom. There you are." I recognized Melissa LeLand once she hurried into the hall and confronted the elderly woman who'd wandered in.

"She's fine!" Iris called back to them. "We are about to open the doors anyways." She gestured for them to come on in.

"I'll go sit by Vince," the elderly woman said, bringing a smile to Melissa's face.

"Hi, Melissa. How are you?" I asked her when she walked up with her mom.

"Mom, this is our mail carrier, Bernadette. This is my mom, Sandra." She began her introductions. "You must be the famous Vince I've heard all about."

"You've not heard all about him." Sandra blushed. It was cute to see an older woman still appreciating an older man's good looks.

Vince was a looker. He also took pride in keeping his body in shape, making him a huge catch around here.

"It's okay. All the residents here talk about him," I teased.

"I heard you were coming back today. Will you be staying in your condo or here in the facility?" Sandra was going to get a leg up on all the ladies.

"I'm in my condo, but it doesn't mean we can't meet for the late-night swim." He winked at her.

"Late-night swim?" I asked, since this was news to me.

"Let's just keep it between us." He gestured between him and Sandra, a sly look on his face.

"There you two are." A male voice interrupted the conversation from a distance. "I've been looking all over for you." Horace LeLand rushed across the floor. He glanced between Vince and me right before looking at his watch. "You two ready? I've got to get back to work."

"Did you find Vivian?" The bite in Melissa's tone didn't go unnoticed. In fact, it took me by surprise.

"No, Melissa." Horace's head flinched just enough to make a strand of his slicked-back hair fall down his forehead. "If you have all the time in the world to run around this place so we can beg to pay for your mother, then you do it. Otherwise, I've got to get back to the station to take care of some more important business, like the kind that does pay for your mother when they come looking for our money."

Horace's jaw clenched, and I couldn't help but notice his balled fists at his sides as he gave his wife a long, hateful stare.

From the looks of it, Melissa was trying to keep her words in her mouth. Her lips were pinched tight.

I busied myself with putting out the ink dabbers on the tables. Normally, we let the residents choose what colors they wanted from the bin when they walked into the dining hall. The argument between Melissa and Horace was so intense I had to find something to do or at least appear to look like I was doing something. In reality, I was listening and keeping one eye on them the entire time.

"I'm sorry, dear." Sandra gave her daughter a slight smile and patted her back. "It'll all work out."

"That man infuriates me. He doesn't care about anyone but himself and that stupid job. I should've left him when I had the chance years ago." A shadow passed over her face, darkening her features. She slid her gaze to the door, where

Horace had already disappeared. "I wish he was gone forever."

"Honey. No you don't. I'm a burden on your marriage. I have been for years." Sandra started to go down the path I'd heard about residents of the senior living facility.

Most of them did struggle with being a burden on their families, but I could see Sandra was not in any way a burden to Melissa.

"Don't you talk like that," Melissa corrected her. "Horace knew years ago before we were married, kids or not, that you were always my number-one priority."

"Kids or not"? The odd statement struck me funny.

"Bernie!" Iris chirped my name over the microphone. "Can you come up here? Now?"

She emphasized "now."

I tilted my head and widened my eyes, giving a little tick gesture toward Melissa and Sandra to let Iris know I was listening in, but she mouthed *now*.

Now it was.

"Do you mind walking around and placing a few colors on each table?" I shoved the box into Melissa's arms. "Unless you need to go."

Melissa looked at her watch. Her brows pinched as she let out a grunting noise like she was about to say something but didn't. She simply took the box and started to do what I'd asked.

When I got to the front, "What do you want?" I asked Iris.

She put the palm of her hand over the microphone and put it down to her side.

"I think there's going to be a storm." Her tired, middle-aged eyes looked at me as if she were in a trance.

"According to Horace's weather report, the day of the wedding is going to be iffy, but I think it's clear this week until then." I wondered why on earth Iris was trying to give me the weather.

"Not that kind of storm." She blinked a few times before her eyes really snapped into focus. "There's going to be a murder."

Chapter 5

"She actually said 'murder'?" Mac Tabor asked from the opposite side of the farm table.

"Murder." I stood up and glanced around to make sure Grady and Julia heard me correctly too. "Mmmm." I phonetically made the *M* sound when I looked at Clara to help with her ever-growing word list. "Mmmm, mur-der."

"Stop it, Mom." Grady sighed. "Clara doesn't need to know about murder."

"Like she's gonna know." I walked around to each of them, reached around, and picked up their plates.

"Don't do that, Bernie. I've got it." Julia tried to stop me.

"You cooked. It's fair Mac and I clean." I shot my soon-to-be husband a look and put the stack of dishes on the kitchen counter.

"There's the look." Mac laughed and got up to join me.

"Mmmmaaa, mmmaaa," Clara clapped and bounced in her high chair.

"See, Clara wants to go outside and swing." I picked up a couple of bowls, which were filled with vegetables, off the table. "Do you want me to keep what is left over?" I asked Julia.

"Yes. Please. There's just enough for Clara to have tomorrow." Julia glanced at Grady. "It's nice to have Grady home for supper and now some time with Clara."

This was Julia's way of thanking him for not having football practice tonight. It was rare for him to be home during suppertime. Julia would feed Clara but wait to eat until Grady got home so they could have dinner together.

"Then you two go enjoy your family. Mac and I have this." I looked at the mound of pots and pans Julia had used.

"Thank you, Bernie." Julia was so grateful. She was just like a daughter to me, and I wanted her and Grady to enjoy little Clara. "Grady?" Julia's voice was so commanding Grady wouldn't even come close to protesting what his wife was telling him.

"Hurry up," he told Mac. "I want to go over the play book with you one last time to see what you think about the opening drive."

"You two can talk business tomorrow." Julia unhooked Clara from the high chair and picked her up. "Right now we are going to take Clara outside to enjoy this wonderful night." Julia put her nose to Clara's. "Isn't Mommy right?"

Clara giggled with joy.

"Look at them." I sighed and looked out the window above the kitchen sink to the back yard. There, Grady and Julia were walking with Clara to the old swing set Richard had built for Grady when he was about Clara's age.

Mac stood behind me. He was so close I could feel the heat from his body radiate.

"I'd much rather be talking to you about our wedding." He bent his lips and kissed my neck. His hands came around from behind me.

Instead of wrapping them around me, he plunged them into the warm soapy water to clean a plate.

"You're all sorts of romantic." I laughed and moved away so he could finish cleaning the plates in the sink before I refilled it with more. "What do you think about what Iris said?"

"I think Iris really wants to believe she has some sort of psychic ability, but from what you said, you two overheard a conversation between an unhappy husband and wife that got a little heated. I'm sure they're fine tonight." Mac picked up the dish towel and tossed it over my shoulder. "Dry."

"Fine." I pulled the towel off my shoulder, took the dripping plate from him, and quickly dried it off.

"Let's talk about something that's important." Mac was surprising me. Whenever I talked or wanted to discuss the wedding, he would simply tell me he was fine with whatever I wanted to do. I just had to tell him a time.

I smiled and walked the plate over to the cabinet where Julia kept them. Grady had made a lot of upgrades since moving in, and Julia had moved all the contents of the cabinet around from when I had lived there. It was fine. Not that I would've put the plates far away from the dishwasher, but this house was her home now. Not what I'd do.

"How about a little music while we talk about what's important?" Mac turned on the raido.

WSCG had so many different programs. Since it was our only local radio station, it played all genres of music and various talk shows throughout the day.

At night, the program was more along the lines of a call-in dedication show, and about ninety percent of the requests were for love songs people wanted dedicated to their loved ones. Perfect for doing dishes, if you asked me. And the love song playing didn't disappoint.

"What would you like to talk about?" I swayed my way over to get another dripping plate from Mac.

"If you think we should call heads or tails during the coin toss?" Mac's question made my jaw drop.

"Mac Tabor." I wound up the towel and flicked it against his thigh.

"Ouch! I'm kidding." He put his soapy hands up in the air and tried to back away from me while I gave him a couple more teasing flicks of the towel.

"Breaking news," the announcer of the radio station said. "Breaking news. Horace LeLand, our beloved meteorologist here at WSCG, has died. We have confirmed from Sheriff Angela Hafley the news about meteorologist and co-worker Horace LeLand. In a statement put out by Vick Morris, the general manager here at WSCG, he called Horace a member of our family as well as the community. Horace was an active member of Sugar Creek Gap in what short time he'd been here, and our condolences go out to his wife, Melissa LeLand, and mother-in-law, Sandra Rothchester. Details about public visitation will be following in the next few days."

"Did you hear that?" I hurried back over to the radio and turned up the volume just in case there was any more news.

My phone rang from inside my purse, which was hanging from the kitchen chair.

"I'll tell Grady and Julia we are leaving." Mac knew me so well.

More than I cared to admit with this situation.

"Iris," I gasped as I quickly cleaned up the kitchen table. "Did you hear about Horace LeLand? Poor guy."

"Yeah. I told you someone was going to be murdered." Iris and her feelings always made me feel a little uncomfortable.

Even after all these years of her predicting strange things that came true—not always but enough for someone to take notice. And I couldn't forget how she'd given me the heads-up about Richard and his car wreck. When I gave in and finally decided to call Richard, I tried several times without getting an answer from him. I figured he was in a meeting, but in reality, he had died. Later that night, when I was sitting in the stands at the high school football game watching Grady run around as the Grizzly mascot, the state police found me and let me know the horrific news.

That didn't even seal the deal how Iris had those feelings I continued to believe were just a case of great women's intuition.

"Are you going to say it or not?" Iris demanded more than questioned.

"Fine." I knew what she wanted to hear. "You were right. Someone died. Not murdered like you said."

"I think being stabbed in your head with a letter opener pretty much qualifies as murder." Iris made my brain and entire body stop. "Bernie? Are you still there? Bernie?"

"Did..." I gulped. "Did..." I gulped twice this time. I sucked in a deep breath and let it rip. "Did you say letter opener?"

"Yep."

"Just like what happened to Vince." The stark realization sank in that Vince's claim that someone tried to murder him had become more than a claim.

It was a reality.

Chapter 6

Main Street was blocked off to any through traffic other than the residents who lived off Short Street and Little Creek Road. Seven p.m. didn't seem so late, but in the fall the sun set much earlier, making seven o'clock feel more like ten o'clock.

"Why do you think it's blocked off?" I rubbernecked to see out the window of his car. Mac didn't have any sort of answer for me. "It looks like all the lights are near the radio station."

Not only the sheriff's car but what looked like every single deputy's car had its lights on, creating a good light show in the darkness.

My scalp prickled when Mac slowly drove the car past WSCG radio station, and I stared past him from the passenger side. The inside of the station was crawling with officers. Angela Hafley was inside talking to Vick Morris, the station manager. She was also speaking to a couple of other people I'd recognized as employees, but I didn't know them.

Mac turned left on Short, giving us a different angle of what things looked like from that side of the building.

"Oh." I gasped when I saw Jigs Baker, the county coroner, sliding what must've been Horace's body underneath a white sheet. "He was killed at the radio station? With a letter opener?"

It was in my nature to try to put things together ever since Richard had died. His death wasn't a mystery. He was killed in a car wreck, but the circumstances surrounding his death were a puzzle. Why was he in that area when he crashed? One thing led to another, and by the time I was finished piecing things together, I'd learned details about my husband, the father of my child, that I never ever would've thought were possible.

I blamed it on that situation that led me to where I was today. Nosy. I was just plain nosy and needed to know things.

Mac didn't like how I inserted myself into matters that were clearly none of my business, and Horace LeLand wasn't really my business, but Vince Caldwell sure was.

"Letter opener?" Mac drove over the bridge crossing Little Creek before he took a left on Little Creek Road then immediately pulled into his driveway.

"Yeah." I unclicked my seat belt and turned toward him. "Iris said he was killed, just like Vince's attempted murder."

"Whoa." Mac gripped the steering wheel and let the car idle. "I thought everyone came to agreement Vince wasn't the target."

"If everyone you mean Angela Hafley, then I can safely say she's probably changed her mind about that." My eyes slid past Mac, and I noticed Harriette, Ruby, Gertrude, and Millie were already on the front porch.

Mac turned and looked to see what got my attention.

"This was a great evening. I'll see you tomorrow." I leaned over and kissed him. "I must go and see what they know."

"You can't be serious, Bernadette." Mac let go of the wheel and rubbed the back of his neck. One of his signs of stress. "Not only is Clara's first birthday this week, and so is the football opener, but we are getting married. Husband and wife. It takes two people present to do that, and when you do your little armchair sleuthing, you get sidetracked, and everything else in your life falls away."

"I would never let those three things fall to the wayside. Besides, we are just talking about it." I knew better than to suggest the Front Porch Ladies and I weren't going to snoop around now that two people had been stabbed with a letter opener. "We are just visiting."

"Mm-hmmm." He lowered his eyes. "You better not miss Clara's birthday, the first punt of the game, and when it's time to say 'I do.'"

"I won't." I gave him one more good kiss before I jumped out of his car. "I'll call you in the morning."

I slammed the door and hurried down his front sidewalk, through his gate, and immediately past Harriette's gate.

"I guess you heard." Harriette had already started to pour a glass of iced tea for me. "Letter opener."

I sat down on the top step, my back resting up against the brick pillar.

"Just like Vince Caldwell said someone tried to kill him." Ruby gave a slow nod, her saggy jowls swaying.

Mac's front door slammed so hard the glass rattled.

We all looked toward his house, and then they all turned to look at me.

"He's not super happy I had to leave Grady's to come home after I heard the news on the radio." I took a sip of the tea. "He told me I better not miss all the things."

"We can talk about this next week." Gertrude was always trying to improve things for everyone.

"No we can't." Harriette and I were on the same page. "Time is important."

"Time?" Millie leaned back in the porch swing and used her toes to slowly rock herself and Ruby back and forth. "Heck, it was a few months ago when they attacked Vince. We at least have a couple of months."

"I wouldn't be so sure." I sat up a little straighter. "What if they had been planning Horace's murder after Vince's was a bust? The killer knew they had to do it right the second time."

"We don't even know if the killer is the same person," Millie groaned.

"It seems a little too convenient to me that it's the same murder weapon." It was something I couldn't let go.

"The real question right now is, What do Vince Caldwell and Horace LeLand have in common?" Harriette Pearl's question made something click in my head.

"Sandra Rothchester," I said, the name floating right out of my mouth. "Horace's mother-in-law."

"I know Sandra," Gertrude said. "She and I are taking the wreath arrangement class together at the Leaf and Petal. She's gotten very close with Sara. It's being hosted by the Elks Women's Club. We meet tomorrow."

"Is Sara Rammond teaching the class?" I asked.

Sara and Larry Rammond owned the local florist.

"She is. We are making the most beautiful fall wreath with silky flowers. They aren't real, which means the wreath will keep season after season." Gertrude's mind had shifted from murder to wreaths. "Sandra needs a little more time, since she has a little arthritis, and Sara is so sweet. She spends extra time after class while everyone is gone so she can help Sandra."

"Where is the meeting, and what is the time?" I wanted to know so I could stop in there. There was no better way of eavesdropping and learning of little pieces of gossip than listening to a bunch of women talk.

"It's at the Elks Club at noon. Why?" Gertrude asked.

"Sara is already on my list of people to see before the wedding, since she and Larry are doing the fall flower arrangements for the tables. I'm guessing Sandra won't be there tomorrow." The death of her son-in-law would seem like a reasonable explanation for missing the class. "I think I'll come to see if Sara has heard Sandra say anything about Horace."

"Do you think she should've?" Gertrude asked.

"Without me going into too much detail, let's just say I don't believe Melissa and Horace had a very good marriage. But I want you four to keep your ears open for any news to why——" My mind stopped my mouth. "Oh my gosh!"

"What? What did you remember?" Harriette eased up on the edge of her rocker.

"I wonder if the killer thought Vince was Sandra." Vince's recollection of his stabbing started to kind of make sense if I twisted it enough. "Vince said his carpet was getting replaced in his condo, so he was staying in the main building. Vince was attacked from behind while he was napping in a chair. I can't help but wonder if the killer thought Vince was Sandra and just stabbed him from behind."

"The only way to find out..." Millie Barnes had a look of fear in her eyes. "Find out where Sandra has stayed in the nursing home. Track her steps."

"I'm worried Sandra LeLand is next." Suddenly the weather shifted, and a cool breeze rolled down the hills and into the holler, making goosebumps crawl up the back of my neck.

"What on earth would they want with an old woman like Sandra?" Ruby raised a good question.

A strange sound echoing down toward my end of the street made us all stop talking. There aren't any lights on Little Creek Road, which made it hard for us to see, but the noise was getting louder by the second.

"What is that?" I squinted and stood up to see if I could get a better look, and I heard something dragging. After a slight pause came a little bang followed up by a squeak. The effect was not only odd but also a little scary.

Just as the sound hit the shadow of the glow of Harriette's

front porch light, a silver walker slammed on the road, creating the little thud. The dragging noise of squeaky wheels followed before the shuffling feet of Vince Caldwell appeared.

"Vince." I set my tea on the porch floor and rushed down the sidewalk, where I met him at Harriette's gate. "What on earth are you doing here?"

"Getting in a little exercise. Isn't that what you wanted me to do?" Vince played my own tactics against me. "Let me have your arm."

I stuck out my arm, and he took it while he shuffled out of the walker, leaving it at the gate.

"Darn thing. It's hell trying to recover from getting murdered." Vince made light of the situation. "That's why I'm here. I tried calling you, but you didn't answer, so I figured it was just as safe taking a nighttime stroll as being a sitting duck for the killer. He couldn't complete the job before, but he's had practice and luck since."

"About that." I let Vince pick the walking pace as we made our way up to the Front Porch Ladies. "We've been talking."

"Of course you five have." He stopped at the steps and looked at them like they were Mount Le Conte, the mountain range in Tennessee that was so hard to climb. "And what did y'all come up with?"

"Vince, let me get you a chair." Harriette hurried into her house, letting the screen door slam shut.

"How are you?" Gertrude asked as she, Ruby, and Millie walked down the steps to give him a proper greeting.

"We've been worried sick." Ruby tsked.

"Bernie has kept us up to date. She's a good one." Millie patted me. "Now with this killer, we do believe you were a victim."

"Glad to see you finally believe me." He slid me a look. "It's funny how people believe this old coot now. Angela came to see me a few hours after that weatherman was found dead."

"Did she now?" I met Harriette on the porch so I could carry the folding chair down for Vince to sit on.

"She sure did." He eased down, and from what I could tell in the dark, he was getting a lot stronger. "I told her the same story about how I didn't see it coming. The person came up from behind me and bludgeoned me. Wanted me dead."

"Did they specifically want you dead?" Harriette had also gotten Vince a glass of iced tea.

"Do you see this?" He pointed at the shaved spot in the back of his head where the killer had stabbed him and the surgeons saved him. "Does that look specific enough for you?"

"What Harriette is asking is, Do you think the killer thought you were someone else?" I saw Vince's confused expression. "You said you were only in there because your carpet was getting replaced. Now that Horace LeLand is dead, the only tie to the senior living facility is Sandra, his mother-in-law. I can't help but wonder if the killer thought the room you were in was actually Sandra's room."

"Bernadette Butler, I think you are on to something." Vince's eyes lowered, and his mouth contorted to the side like he was really thinking about the scenario. "Come to think of it, that is the room Vivian uses for residents when they have something done to their place or if they are waiting for a transfer."

"Would Vivian know who had stayed in there?" Millie asked.

"She should, and you know, I do believe Sandra stayed in there because the morning of my near murder, Melissa walked in while I was watching *The Price Is Right*. She was surprised to see me in there and apologized. I didn't think anything of it, since they were pretty new to the place. I just thought she was lost." Vince had uncovered some important information that sounded like it needed to be written down. "Do you think Melissa is behind this?"

"The spouse is always a suspect." Ruby Dean must've

turned up her ears because she was all into the conversation, and no one had to repeat themselves.

"The spouse—but her mom?" I questioned Melissa's motive. "Though I did hear her say something today about Horace needing to see Vivian. Do you know what that was about?"

"Or what it could be about?" Harriette brought the glass pitcher down and refilled everyone's glass, a sure sign we were going to be here for a little while longer.

By this time, the Front Porch ladies and I were all snugged up on Harriette's front porch steps, facing Vince's folding chair.

"I don't know, but I did find it odd they were arguing. You were standing there. You didn't hear them?" he asked me.

"I think I was just shocked they were arguing in front of us. I didn't pay attention to what the argument was about, but the one thing I did walk away thinking was Melissa and Horace's marriage wasn't all that great." I hated to say it, but the way they were fussing made me believe they had their fair share of problems. "Wait. Money."

"You think they were having money problems?" Gertrude asked.

"I don't know, but I do remember Horace saying something about when payment was due, he would bet Vivian would be hunting them down or something like that." I had completely forgotten Horace saying something about Sandra's payment.

"Now we have a motive." Ruby's cheeks balled as her grin grew.

"We have a motive for Melissa to have been mad enough at Horace if he didn't pay or whatever it was about." Another question I was sure to ask Vivian when I stopped in and saw her tomorrow. "But why would she attempt to kill her mom?"

"Maybe she didn't. Maybe Horace and Melissa knew her mom was in the holdover room where Vince was, and she knew someone had tried to kill Vince." Harriette's brows rose. "Let's face it. Vince hasn't been quiet about that little fact."

"Instead of giving Horace the opportunity to try to kill Sandra again, Melissa got to him first." Gertrude brushed her hands together as if she were finishing the deed.

"Let me get this straight." I had to work it all out in my head, so when I went to see Vivian I could ask the correct questions before letting Angela Hafley in on the motives and the killer. It wasn't like Angela was asking for my help, but I saw things no one but a mail carrier was privy to. In this case, it was just information falling into my lap, and if I could help, I would.

For me to enjoy Clara's birthday party, the big football game, and my wedding, this case needed to be wrapped up before any of them. I was on a mission.

"Sandra Rothchester moved into the holdover room in the senior living facility because there wasn't a room available yet. We believe Horace and Melissa pay for Sandra to live there. Horace attempted to kill Sandra so he wouldn't have to pay, but instead he stabbed the wrong person." I pointed at Vince. "In this case, it was Vince Caldwell."

"Horace messed with the wrong man on this one." Vince Caldwell's confidence was coming back in full force, and I loved it.

"Yeah, he did." Ruby batted her lashes. Gertrude back-handed Ruby's arm. "Ouch." Ruby tried to rub out the sting.

"This is no time for goo-goo eyes." Gertrude reminded Ruby, who glared.

"Vince's attempted murder made Melissa think about how it could've been her own mother if it'd been a day earlier, but she began to put two and two together. She kept on Horace about payment and knew he had tried to kill her mother over the money."

"Greed is a good motive." Harriette sipped her iced tea.

"That's when she plotted to kill Horace." I let that hang in silence while we all wet our whistles.

"But if he's dead, how's she gonna pay for Sandra?" Millie asked. We all looked around at one another for the answer.

"Maybe Horace had a good insurance policy?" Gertrude shrugged. The ice in her glass clinked the sides as she took another drink.

"And Melissa would be the beneficiary, since she is his wife. With the money, she could easily pay for her mom's care without the headache of going to Horace each time." It all sounded like a really good reason for Melissa LeLand to kill her husband and for Horace to have attempted to kill Sandra Rothchester, his mother-in-law.

My theory had many speculations that would be easy to prove, and I knew if I was going to start digging in for those answers tomorrow, I had to get a good night's sleep.

Chapter 7

I'd love to say getting the much-needed good night's sleep was exactly what I did, but in reality, my mind was swirling with questions surrounding the attempted murder of Vince and the actual murder of Horace.

I'd even made some notes on my phone app to share with Iris, since I would stop in her place for a late-morning snack and discuss what Vince, the Front Porch Ladies, and I had uncovered. Plus, Iris loved the snooping stuff, and she enjoyed staring at and writing on the little whiteboard in her bakery while she was baking. She said things would come to her from the freedom of being creative.

I had no clue what that meant but whatever. Iris had been her own odd bird since I knew her, and it was fine with me. That was what made me love her even more. Her crazy side.

"Here you go." Rowena had curled her long orange tail around my shin as I stood at the back door waiting for Buster to go potty. I dumped some kibble in her bowl.

She ran over to gobble it up because she knew if she didn't, Buster would. He preferred her food over his kibble.

Little did she ever remember how I would simply put her

bowl up on the kitchen counter so he couldn't jump up there like she could and eat her food in peace.

The coffee pot beeped, indicating the brewing was finished, and I moved away from watching Rowena enjoy her food. I grabbed my first cup of coffee and headed outside to see what was taking Buster so long.

The darkness and chill surrounded me. The eerie silence of the early morning mixed with Buster's paws crunching the grass while he had his nose to the ground along the fence line, sniffing all the new smells created overnight.

I sat down on my patio chair and peeled the soft blanket off the back of the chair to cover my legs. It was going to be a cool fall day, which meant long work pants for me and bringing extra treats along the way. Not only for my duck friend but my customers.

The day would be perfect for chitchat, and it wasn't just because the weather brought people out. It was because there was a murder along my route, and they would want to know exactly what I knew. Vice versa for me.

The theory about Horace's death we'd come up with last night did seem plausible, and much stranger things had happened in order for people to kill others. That knowledge kept me from sleeping. It seemed too easy to figure out, and was that the case here?

A daughter who simply wanted her mother to be taken care of? Did Horace promise this to Melissa all these years, and when it happened, did he go back? Had something happened recently to their finances that prevented him from making good on his promise to his wife to take care of her mother?

So many questions needed to be answered for me before I could even bring them up to Angela Hafley.

Sitting here sipping coffee wouldn't get me those answers.

"Let's eat, Buster." I clicked my tongue and stood up,

folding the blanket back over the chair so it would be ready for me later.

My phone was ringing when I walked inside.

"What took you so long?" Mac's tone contained a bit of panic. "I was about to run down there."

"I was outside with Buster." It sounded funny that Mac would think I wasn't safe. "Are you okay?"

"Anytime there's a murder close to our house and they haven't caught the killer, I'm a little concerned for your safety." Mac had always been such a good guy from the moment I'd met him.

Richard had introduced me to Mac. They were college roommates, and I'd always questioned why Mac had never gotten married. He was kind, considerate, full of manners, and good-looking, and he had a smile that would rocket your heart straight into orbit before you even realized it'd left your body.

Years later, Mac confessed he'd fallen for me with one look when Richard first introduced us and that he knew he could never give half a heart to a woman. It wasn't like Mac swooped in and took my heart after Richard died. It was a lot more complicated than that, but the natural transition we'd made from friends to lovers was pretty seamless. He'd already been an uncle-type figure to Grady and even stepped into the father role when Richard passed.

He loved me for me. He'd never tried to change me. He'd never told me to stop snooping around. He'd never told me anything but "I love you." And I couldn't wait until we were living under the same roof as husband and wife.

I looked down at the ring on my finger and smiled.

"I'm fine. I love you for how you care so much, though." For a moment, I forgot about the murder and dreamed of what it would look like in a few days, when we would both stand at the farm proclaiming our life as a married couple in front of friends and family. "Did you and Grady go for your final tux fitting?"

"That's today. I've also got to grab your dad, and I don't want your mom to start talking about the cakes." Mac was as exhausted as I was about Mom and her carrying on about the gluten-free menu.

"Have Grady go in. I don't think she has the nerve to say something to him. Just us. Like we can do anything. But I'll see if Iris can make Mom a sample of Clara's gluten-free apple pie. It looked really good yesterday." I thought if Mom could get a sample and see how good it was, she'd change her mind.

"Do you want me to walk you to the post office this morning?" he asked, even though I knew it wasn't because he wanted to spend the time. It was because it was cold and dark, and I'd be alone.

"It's not that far. Just over the bridge and across the street." It sounded as close as it was. The post office was literally the first building in the heart of Main Street. "I promise to carry my heavy flashlight."

It was more of a weapon because it was so heavy I knew I could give someone a good whack. As a mail carrier, I encountered a lot of hostile customers. With the informational emails, delivery customers knew what was coming to the mailbox before I even showed up. When the awaited piece of mail wasn't put into my stack and I didn't have it with me, the customer would get disgruntled, letting me know their email told them the mail they wanted was coming today.

Monthly state checks, child support, and even magazine subscriptions were highly anticipated pieces of mail.

"How about lunch today?" I asked Mac as I walked down the hall with another full mug of coffee so I could slip into my long-pants mail carrier uniform. "I'm going to be driving the LLV for the third loop so we can meet and stop by the Elks because Sara will be there for her wreath making class. It'll be easier to stop in there instead of driving out to the Leaf and Petal."

"Since you're going to go anyways to ask some questions, I guess I'll go with you." Mac's voice had returned to normal, not frantic. "I've got Julia turning in the final project proposal we've been working on, so I'm going to give her the afternoon off. You know, I really wish she'd go back to college and get her architecture licenses. I'd love to give the business to her."

"I think right now she's too busy trying to make the babies to even think about anything else." I wanted Julia and Grady's wishes to come true so bad. "Besides, her business degree helps you just fine for now."

Julia and Grady had met in college. Julia had graduated with a business degree and Grady with his teaching certificate, though his real dream was to be on the football field as the head coach.

Grady had an eye for football and easily got a job at Sugar Creek Gap High School as a member of the coaching staff. His dream to be offered the position of head coach happened pretty fast, so to say it was nothing short of exciting was an understatement. His dreams were coming true. He'd gotten the job he'd always wanted, the woman of his heart, and a sweet baby girl.

This new dream of adding to his family and the reality of it never coming true hurt my heart now.

As a mother, it was hard to not see all your child's dreams come to life. No matter how hard Julia and Grady had tried to have another baby, there was one obstacle after another. The one issue with Grady and his frustration surrounding the matter was that he couldn't make things happen.

"Hopefully, football will help keep things off Grady's mind." Mac sighed. "Speaking of which, what's new with the boosters?"

"You know the same. We will have our annual Christmas

tree fundraiser. Don't forget to remind me to talk to Sara about that today too." The Christmas tree fundraiser was a huge moneymaker for the football program.

The ability to offer donors a freshly cut Christmas tree from the Rammonds' tree farm was such a blessing.

"I've got to get ready. I'll text you to let you know I made it to the post office. I love you," I told him. We said our goodbyes.

Rowena had already curled back up in the bed on the pillow, and Buster had found his spot in the corner of the couch, not caring a bit I was about to leave. Some days Buster liked to tag along with me, and other days he didn't. He'd start wanting to go more now that the weather was changing.

I grabbed the mailbag with only the bag of duck feed in it and headed out the door. There was no life on Little Creek Road this early in the morning. When I made it to Main Street, I found the same there. Nothing.

I looked down toward the radio station. Long gone were the flashing lights from last night. I hurried across Main Street and walked through the parking lot of the post office to the back lot, where all the LLVs were lined up, started, and ready to go.

A few of the carriers were already walking around their LLVs, holding clipboards and checking off their daily mechanical lists. These things were called Lifelong Vehicles for a reason. The post office just kept putting Band-Aids on them when we really needed an entirely new fleet.

"Good morning, Bernie!" Monica Reed greeted me with excitement. She was a clerk who worked the counter inside the post office, and she got there just as early as the rest of us. If she had time in the morning, she would help sort through all the mail. She was good at it. "I think you're going to have a very busy, chatty day."

"I think so too." I took the stack of mail she'd already separated for my first loop and tossed it into my bag. "I have a bunch of my own questions."

I looked in the bin with all the mail that was considered junk and tried to pick out a few generic pieces I could have in hand for Vivian Tillett, since I had to have some sort of excuse to see her.

Mail was always a great one. Vivian would see right through it, but it felt better to me.

"I can't wait to hear what the word on the street is." Monica glanced up when someone called her name. "Take plenty of notes. And I'm excited about the wedding."

"Me too." Satisfied with the stack of junk mail, I grabbed a rubber band and banded the pieces together. Then I put the bound mail in the front pocket so I knew exactly where to grab it once I found Vivian.

The senior living facility was always the first loop on my deliveries. Not because it was right behind the post office but because most residents, except for Vince, would be asleep. My customers there all loved to talk. I had a hard time cutting them off and excusing myself so I didn't put myself in their situations. Volunteering let me scratch the itch to give myself permission to put them first, but today I had to go inside the facility, not just the mail room. (The mail room had rows upon rows of small metal mailboxes. In there, I could easily go down the line there, tossing pieces of mail in each box.)

"Fancy seeing you up so early." I greeted Vince at the front porch of the main building, where he was always sitting on the swing with his cup of coffee and newspaper. "Anything new since a few hours ago?" I asked.

"Not a thing. Not even much in the paper but an ongoing investigation. Jigs is expected to finish the autopsy report and release the body for burial." Vince snapped the paper taut to read me a little bit of the headline. "Are we sticking to the plan?"

"Yep. I'm going to go find Vivian now." I pulled the banded stack of junk mail I was using as a decoy out of the front pocket of my mailbag. "Here is my way in."

"She's in her office. I already scouted it out." Vince crumbled the paper back a little so he could look at me. "I've been thinking."

"You mean you've been up all night researching?" It was my way of asking if he'd used his contacts to look up anyone or anything. Namely Horace LeLand.

"Both. Up all night thinking about your theory, and it's a good one. I do think someone thought Sandra was in there. The more I've been unable to recall the ten minutes before the stabbing or the few days after, but I can remember where I was sitting, and my back was to the door. I'd asked Vivian to bring me a chair with a straighter back." His eyes darkened. His face stilled as though he were replaying the events in his head. "She had one of the orderlies bring one of the wingbacks with a really tall back from the sitting room. I remember leaning my head back, and it didn't even clear the top, which was actually kinda nice and pillowy."

The sun started to peek over the hills in the background. The morning dew left by the chill of the night would soon melt away and leave us with a sunny day but a little nip to the air.

Vince looked out past the parking lot. The new sunrays cast an orange glow on his face.

"I remember thinking it would be nice to have a chair this high in my condo. That's it. After that I don't recall. But the importance of me remembering the chair was that if you walked into the room, you would barely see the top of my head." His voice trailed off, sounding weak.

"Making it easy for someone to think it was Sandra," I said, finishing his sentence. "And this is why I don't want you snooping around. You need to continue to rest, sleep, and gain your strength back."

"I'll be fine." He coughed a couple of times. "I did get in contact with one of my old colleagues who has been able to look into any sort of finances Horace had or left behind. Nothing out of the ordinary. It seems like Melissa and he had separate accounts, and his final will had his life insurance going to a grant for college students who were going to school for broadcasting."

"Any loopholes for Melissa to have been able to get her hands on it?" I asked.

"Nothing that would be easy. But she's definitely not independently wealthy. Enough for her to live but not pay the price it costs for Sandra to be here." With that, Vince gave me the motive I needed to explore the possibility that Melissa had killed Horace. Vince added, "Why would she kill her own mother or try to?"

"I don't know. Maybe the financial burden was putting a strain on her marriage. Horace possibly put two and two together with you and confronted her. He found out she tried to kill her own mother and was going to use it against her." These theories were so wild that I couldn't imagine anything like that ever happening, but again, I'd seen murders with less reasoning behind them.

"I guess we won't know what is really going on until I talk to Vivian. One thing I do know is that I want you to go and get some rest. Lock your doors. Sleep. Or you won't be strong enough to participate in all the fun activities coming up in a couple of days." Vince never missed a football game.

Like the rest of the town, he lived for the fall sport and loved to hang on the fence of the football field with my dad and their friends, discussing each play as it happened. They also gave their two cents and groaned when a play didn't go well.

"You won't have the energy to stand for the full game if you don't get some sleep," I warned.

"You're harder than the nurses. You know that?" he asked with a slight smile and got up, giving in to my suggestion. "But you're right. I don't want to miss the game. Or not be mentally alert enough to help you get to the bottom of this murder."

"I've got some dummy mail for Vivian so I have an excuse to get in front of her, so I'm going to go find her. You go back home." We both rose from the swing, and I told him I'd check on him later.

"Keep me posted," he called and started to make his way along the front of the facility toward the independent living condo section where he lived.

The inside of the senior living facility was so nice. Just inside the door sat a reception desk with all the sign-in sheets. It was too early for someone sitting there but soon the place would be bustling with visitors.

The facility had a movie theater, an indoor swimming pool, a workout room, a salon, a couple of cafes, and a library for everyone to enjoy.

It was a really nice place to live. As I walked through the building to get to the offices where Vince said I could find Vivian, the dollar signs ticked up in my mind. The cost of Sandra's living expenses now seemed more like a possible motive for murder.

"Knock knock." I gently hit the dummy stack of mail on the office door when I saw Vivian was in there.

Vivian was in her late twenties and pretty young for her position. She was married to Gill, and at a fairly young age, they had had a daughter.

"Come on in." She looked a little disheveled. Her dark hair, which she had pulled up today, always looked a little unruly.

"Oh, new blond highlights?" I couldn't help but notice. She nodded. "Looks good."

"Goodness, Bernie. You are sweet, but this place is literally killing me. I'm at a loss for words over the new information. The sheriff believes Vince Caldwell was a target of a killer." She put her head in her hands. "A killer."

"Yeah. I heard." I walked in and took the rubber band off the dummy mail, which I set on her desk. "About that."

I took the liberty of sitting down in the seat in front of her desk while she busied herself with thumbing through the stack of mail.

"Junk." She tossed the first one in the trash can. "Junk, junk, and junk."

No surprise to me, she tossed it all.

"It has to cost more for these companies to send out this junk than to simply not send it out." She shook her head.

"We say that all the time at the post office." It was true. The thousands of dollars companies spent on the junk they sent out was amazing to us, but we still delivered it.

"I guess it keeps you in a job," she teased with a smile.

"You know Vince and I are very close." I didn't need to tell her something she already knew, but it was my way of leading into my questions about Sandra. "But I can't let something like someone trying to kill him just pass by. You and I both know I'm going to look into it."

"I thought as much. When I noticed him slipping in and out of the office halls, I thought he might be looking for me, for you." She pointed at the trash. "That's what's up with the junk mail that doesn't have the facility address on it."

"I should've just come out and said what I wanted, huh?" I waited for her to confirm then continued, "I can't help but wonder if the killer mistook Vince for Sandra."

"You think someone was trying to kill Sandra?" Her look of shock quickly fell away to an "oh my gosh, I bet you're right" look of realization. "It was where she was staying."

"Vince also mentioned the chair and how no one coming in the room could really see who was sitting in it." The details of the situation as I told them changed her expression. "I'm not sure why someone would want Sandra dead, and I hate to speculate if it was Melissa or Horace, but I'd like to know what type of payment arrangement Sandra has here."

"I couldn't imagine either of them trying or wanting to kill her. Horace is the one who pays the bill. When they first came to look at the facility after he'd taken the job at WSCG, they thought the price was steep and argued whether Sandra should be in the care center or the independent living area." She let go of a long sigh. "I remember they were so confused about why the care center was more expensive than the independent, and when I told them, they'd both agreed they felt uncomfortable with Sandra living alone with no supervision."

"But she doesn't seem to have any restrictions to keep her here in this care center." I didn't notice anything that would have indicated otherwise when she came to bingo the other day.

"Getting into the care facility takes a while. Years, in fact. We don't have enough rooms for the demand, and once you are in, you're in. They said they'd rather get her in now instead of waiting. Which was why she was in the holdover room for so long. It took those months for a room to come available." Vivian frowned.

"The other day, I overheard Melissa and Horace arguing about the payment. He was never late?" I wanted to make sure I'd heard her correctly.

"Never. Never beforehand either. Right on time. Melissa would call and call leading up to the late-fee deadline to make sure he paid. That's when I knew they didn't share a joint account because she'd said something about not being able to see if the payment was made, and she apologized for calling." Vivian typed on the computer's keyboard. The glow of the backlight glistened on her face. "I told her I'd definitely let them know if he was ever late, hoping she'd stop calling me daily from the first of the month to the eighth. But it didn't. She still called."

Vivian swiveled the computer's monitor around and showed me detailed phone records of calls from family members.

"Wow." I drew back, shocked at what I saw. "She did call every day."

"Like clockwork. She wanted to make sure her mom was taken well care of." She turned the monitor back to its normal position. "We have to keep details of every single thing that happens here. The only thing I can remember Horace saying once was how I'd get his payment every month unless they moved or she died."

"He did?" I was a bit taken back. "That brings me to wonder if Horace had wanted to stop the payments."

Without saying it, I pretty much said he tried to kill Sandra and, in the attempt, accidentally tried to kill Vince.

"You'd think it would be him, but he knew Sandra had moved into her new room a few days prior to Vince's attack." That didn't help my theory. "I'm afraid Horace might look like he had a motive, and I guess he did, but he helped Sandra move into her new place."

And with that, I knew Horace wasn't the one who attacked or mistakenly thought Vince was Sandra, so I was back to square one and wondered why on earth someone would want Sandra dead.

Or Vince?

Chapter 8

"You think you have everything?" Grady called me every morning on his way into work, and today was no different.

He'd called just as I was leaving the post office to pick up my second loop of deliveries. Briefly, I stopped to watch and listen to the babbling brook flowing across the rocks as the old mill pushed the water down the creek. Then I crossed Main Street to start delivering to the local shops.

Hearing Grady call me made my day. Some mornings, he simply said hello, while other conversations were a little longer. This week, we had a lot to talk about.

"Julia said she's got it all covered." He sounded pretty sure about all the arrangements and things necessary for Clara's first birthday party, which was in a couple of days. "And the tents were delivered for the wedding."

"Thank you so much for thinking about the weather." I recalled talking to Grady earlier in the week about Horace's weather forecast. Maybe his last one I'd heard.

"Yeah, we don't want people getting wet if there is a popup." In the background, Grady was fumbling around in his car. Crunching papers and rattle of keys meant he was already at the school. "I guess you heard about the weather guy, right?"

"Mm-hmmm." I bit my lips.

"What does that mean?" he asked. The movement on his end stopped. "Mom."

"Grady."

"Geesh, Mom. Are you kidding me? Are you really thinking you need to stick your nose into this, especially this week?" Grady always scolded me for snooping. "You don't have time for this. Clara's party is on Thursday. Friday is the big game. Saturday is your big day. You should be focusing on, I don't know, decorating or something."

"That's what I don't need to focus on. I need something just like this murder to keep my mind occupied so I don't bother Julia to see if I can do anything. Or worry about the big game rivalry or the weather for my big day."

"We will talk later. Love you." He hung up the phone before I could say "I love you" back, but it was fine, because Grady was well aware of how much I loved him.

With my whole heart.

I had to backtrack to the doctors' office, which was next to the post office, to deliver their mail. That mail took up most of the space in my bag for the second loop. But once it was all delivered, I made my way across to the bank. They rarely had a lot of mail, since they kept a post office box and checked it daily. Then the fun was delivering daily to the local shops. It was like clockwork.

I'd been able to time my morning perfectly for when the shops opened. Most of the time, Leotta at the yarn shop was mainly available to talk, but today she was hosting her weekly knitting class for beginners. She simply waved as I quickly exchanged the outgoing mail with the incoming pieces.

Tranquility Spa was the next small shop on my mail route. Peaches Partin was the owner, and I rarely got the opportunity to talk to her. The establishment was not only a spa but also a yoga studio.

Peaches offered a wakeup yoga class, so while the students were getting their Zen on, I was slipping in and out. I did love the spa, and as my body had started to process all things menopause related, doing yoga and mindful meditation did help relieve some of the stress.

Pie in the Face was the next business, and Iris was busy taking a new custom order on the phone, so I mouthed that I'd stop in later to chat. She nodded at me and went back to writing down the particulars of the order on her notepad.

And today the Wallflower Diner was buzzing with the excitement of what had taken place a few hours ago a couple of shops down.

The restaurant was a typical diner with metal tables and red vinyl metal chairs that took up the interior flooring. The tables had saltshakers filled with salt and a few pieces of elbow macaroni—which kept the salt fresh, according to my mom—along with matching pepper shakers. Fresh cream also lay on the tables for the coffee drinkers. Each table had a small bud vase with a plastic red rose, and the menu was pushed between the bud vase and shakers. Today those creamer pitchers were all being used up as the town folk gathered to drink the coffee and gossip about the weatherman's death.

"Any more news?" I asked Mom, handing her the bundled mail in exchange for a hot biscuit and egg sandwich. I was actually a little early, since Leotta wasn't able to talk, so I took advantage and sat down to enjoy the biscuit and hot cup of coffee Mom had set down in front of me.

"Not a thing. Angela is hush lipped." Mom rolled her eyes. "What on earth is going on? From what I hear, it was a letter opener, just like Vince." She leaned on the counter and whispered, "I told your father that we need to move right back upstairs where we belong. Get out of that retirement facility.

I'm afraid someone is going to be lurking in the darkness and stab us."

"Don't you two still park in your garage?" I wanted to make sure, even though I knew they sometimes rode their bikes to the diner in the morning.

"We do, but that doesn't matter. Vince was inside when they took a swipe at him." Mom's imagination was running wild, just like the rest of the people in the diner. "I heard it was someone in the insurance department somehow making good on dead people's money. Or what if it's the nursing home? You know a lot of people leave their money to places like that."

"Now I think you're going overboard." Even though Mom had good reasons to be concerned, she didn't know the two events had one common denominator.

Sandra Rothchester.

"I'm sure Angela is on it." I didn't tell Mom that I was looking into things. Nothing good ever came of telling her, and she'd just worry herself sick like she was worried about the gluten-free pie.

There was no reason to get my parents involved other than to assure Mom she and Dad weren't the targets of a killer on the loose.

"If it makes you feel any better, I did stop in and say hello to Vivian today to make sure they were being very vigilant about the property. They are." A little bit of relief settled in Mom's eyes when I told her. "And this hit the spot. Thank you."

"Let me get you a to-go cup for your coffee. You look tired." Mom was never one to hold back. "Have you not been sleeping? Who could blame you? Your granddaughter is growing up to be some sort of vegan something or other. I never thought I'd see the day when one of our own didn't eat a biscuit on their first birthday."

"You are making me stressed." I pointed at the fifty-year-old bags under my eyes. "You are stressing me out thinking about Clara. She's fine. She's healthy, and I'm going to do what my son and daughter-in-law feel are best for her. If the doctor thinks Clara needs a different food preference, then they will tell Julia and Grady."

"It just ain't right." Mom poured coffee in a to-go cup and ran her fingers along the edge of the lid to make sure it was sealed. "Did you like your biscuit just now?"

"Yes. I told you it was good." I picked up the cup.

"See. Clara is missing out." Luckily, Mom was cut off by a breaking news alert from Sheriff Angela Hafley.

Hushed whispers ran across the room as all eyes turned to watch the small television that hung on the wall behind the counter. Mom rushed over next to the register and grabbed the remote. She pointed it at the TV and turned up the volume as loud as it would go.

On the news, Angela told the media there weren't any suspects as of right now and pleaded with the community to send in any tips they might have. My phone chirped with a text. Giving me a good reason to leave.

My text was from Iris. She said she was finished with her customer, so I should come back and discuss last night since we'd yet to talk about it. We'd sent a few text messages back and forth throughout the night, but we had not yet talked in person.

"I told you. I told you. I told you." Iris held her fist against her belly. "I told you there was going to be a murder."

"Yes you did." I watched her grab the whiteboard and drag a damp paper towel across the front, cleaning off one of the recipes she'd been working on.

"Now. What do we know?" She wrote Horace's name in the middle of the board. "Besides the fight between him and Melissa."

She drew a line from Horace's name out to the right and wrote Melissa.

"They could've been fighting over money." I filled her in on the theory Vince and I had come up with. That Vince was mistaken for Sandra seemed to light Iris up. "Do you think Melissa put it together and confronted Horace?"

"Why would he kill her? Because he didn't want to pay for her?" There was more to this I'd yet to discover. "I plan on getting in front of Lucy Drake this morning."

"Not without some pumpkin sugar cookies." Iris looked over her shoulder at one of the bakery's industrial ovens. "Lucy Drake's lips get loose when she eats them. Better than slipping her a micky."

Iris was so sneaky. That was why I loved her.

She bent down and looked in the oven's window before she seemed satisfied enough to pull them out.

"We will give them a few minutes to cool, and I'll box them up." She sighed with a smile. "Do you think Melissa LeLand would accept some?"

"It's worth a try. And she wouldn't be expecting anything different, since it's part of our southern hospitality." Taking food to people during big moments in life—in this case, the murder of someone's husband—was as normal as breathing. No questions would be asked, and it would get me in the door of their house.

If I played my cards right, that meant I would get there while a lot of other people were giving Melissa their condolences. I hoped I'd hear something that could spark the discovery of some clues. Even if Melissa didn't kill Horace, maybe she had an inkling who did.

"I'm also going to need some cookies for the Elks. Sara is hosting a wreath class this afternoon, and Sandra is a participant. I'm sure she might have something to say about all of this." I was banking on her being in the class. Even if she wasn't, I was sure Sara Rammond had to know something, since Sara had spent some time alone with Sandra to help with the arthritis.

"All in the name of justice." Iris happily sighed at an excuse to give away more of her hard work. "Enough about all the murder-y stuff. While we wait for them to cool, let's talk about the lovey stuff and your wedding cake."

Chapter 9

"All in the name of justice" wasn't a good excuse to eat all three slices of the cake Iris had baked samples of for the wedding. The three slices covered plain chocolate, which was my favorite, Mac's request for red velvet, and the gluten-free vanilla for Clara.

She couldn't have gone wrong with any of them as crowd pleasers, and no matter what, I knew she'd decorate them elegantly.

At first, I had protested the idea of having a traditional wedding with the big cake, DJ, and fanfare that went along with it. To be fair to Mac, this wedding would be his first, and he wanted all the things, which surprised me. If I had to really guess his thinking behind it, though, I was sure he was saying those things to make me feel better.

The RVSPs had poured in, and I didn't recall seeing one for Lucy Drake, which gave me a good excuse to stop in during her on airtime.

She sat in the big DJ chair with a small set of earphones, the microphone at her lips as she read from a piece of paper in her hand. The outside speakers weren't on, which was unusual because WSCG loved for listeners to gather outside of the station windows and watch the broadcasts live.

I stood outside, waiting for Lucy to finish reading the script. When I felt like she'd rolled to a commercial or a new song, I walked up in her peripheral vision and shook the small bag with a few of Iris's fresh-out-of-the-oven Pumpkin Sugar Cookies.

Lucy held up her finger and spoke into the microphone before she hit a couple of keys, which really sent the listeners to a break this time. Then she emerged from the building.

"Pumpkin Sugar Cookies fresh out of the oven." I jiggled the bag. "And I've yet to get your RSVP to the wedding."

"I'd love to think you came here for my RSVP, but if I know Bernadette Butler, you're wondering about Horace LeLand." She tossed me a knowing look.

"So you caught me." I held the bag out. Reluctantly, she looked at it. "Go on. You know you want one or five."

She took the bag and opened it. With her nose stuck down inside, she took a long whiff.

"I love Pie in the Face in the fall." Lucy happily sighed and stuck her hand in. "I'm not really sure what there is to know."

"Just the particulars." I put my mailbag between my feet as I rested it on the sidewalk to take the load off my shoulder. I reached up and began to knead the tender area. "What was his marriage like? And did you know anyone who would want him or his mother-in-law dead?"

"Sandra?" Lucy was genuinely shocked. She took a step back and blinked a few times as though trying to wrap her head around my question. "Why on earth would anyone want to hurt Sandra? She's the sweetest."

"This is just my theory, but I think someone mistook Vince for Sandra when he was stabbed with the letter opener." I didn't have to go into the particulars with her for her to accept the theory.

Instead, I just had to remember I had two ears and one mouth. Keeping the mouth shut just long enough to create an uncomfortable silence was always my go-to when it came to Lucy Drake. To her, the silence was like dead air on the radio, and it shouldn't be there.

"I can't say for certain about who I think would kill Horace, but there's plenty of motive." She pressed her lips together like she was thinking about what to say next. "If I had to guess, I'd say Angela needs to be checking out Levi Horn."

"Levi Horn? The weekend guy? The football announcer? The guy who is going to do the DJing at my wedding?" I would've never pegged sweet Levi Horn, the weekend weather DJ, as anything but nice and kind. "He always gave me compliments on my delivery on Saturdays. That's when I had the opportunity to hire him to DJ the wedding."

My brows knitted. I had to ask Mac if Levi would still be able to play our music.

"You aren't a threat. Or in the way for anyone around here to climb the ladder." Lucy did have the inside scoop, which was exactly the information I needed. "When Vick hired Horace, he blew the budget for three years. With the crazy cost of living always going up, there's not been any sort of bonuses for gaining new listeners. All the junkets have stopped."

"I did notice Vick didn't make the usual donation to the football boosters." I'd been so busy with planning the wedding I'd let the donations slip a little, but Vick always paid so they could host the football games live and conduct interviews of both the locker-room pre-game and exclusive, on-air post-game varieties.

"Vick took all of that away this year. There's not going to be any coverage of the games, recorded or live. Nothing." I stood there pretty much shocked.

"The people of Sugar Creek Gap will not stand for that." Obviously, no one knew about it other than the employees of the radio station. "Where are they ever going to announce this information? What about Levi?"

"This is why I think Levi had the best motive to knock off Horace." She didn't seem in the least bit bothered by the idea that one of her co-workers would off another co-worker. "And I don't blame him."

"Lucy," I gasped.

"We all got a raw deal when Vick hired Horace. It wasn't in the budget. I would go to all the local events. My morning talk show pretty much ended because Horace insisted on doing those morning live weather broadcasts. Vick implemented the new weather alert system that spits out the weather far enough in advance that Levi was to record his weekend forecasts."

"I didn't even realize they were recorded." I did recall not seeing Levi in the DJ booth a couple of consecutive weeks here and there, but I never gave it too much thought.

"Yep. All pre-recorded unless there was an unexpected weather event. Vick had given Horace the reins on deciding if he wanted to come in on those occasions or have Levi come in. Only Levi didn't get any more compensation for coming in." She shook her head. "Now Vick has taken away the football games to continue to pay for Horace's yearly bonus, which means no donations to anything other than Horace's bank account."

All this news was so shocking and disappointing at the same time.

"Are you going to be featuring all of this on your crime show?" I wondered just how far she'd go with the details. "I mean, you've already featured a couple of the cases here in Sugar Creek Gap. I'm assuming a good reporter like you wouldn't stop just because it's in your own backyard."

Lucy Drake loved compliments. Calling her a reporter was a far cry from the truth. Recently, she'd dipped her toe into the growing and popular crime-podcast-type programs, and she took full advantage of her DJ platform to help promote her efforts.

"Do you think Vick is going to let me have special privileges and pay me to work on Sunday?" Her face showed no emotions. Flat. "When I tell you Levi's reports are recorded, the entire show on Sunday is just on autopilot. Listen to it this week. You'll notice it's all music all day long with as many ads in between."

"I sure hate to hear that. Mac and I enjoyed listening to you bring all those crimes to life." It was something Mac and I enjoyed after church on Sunday. Even Iris would join us on occasion, and we'd take turns trying to figure out whodunit. "If there are ads being run, aren't those paying for a lot of the salaries?"

"You'd think Vick would be smart enough not to raise the cost of a thirty-second ad, but when he hired Horace, he tripled the cost, saying advertisers would pay to have Horace mention their names." My stomach lurched with Lucy's comment.

"Business owners have pulled advertising?" I tried to recall the last time I'd heard an advertisement on WSCG. Mainly, I kept the station on for background noise.

"Have you heard anything from Kenneth Simpson lately?" she asked, referring to the pro golfer at Sugar Creek Gap Country Club. "He was a regular, advertising golf lessons, summer golf lessons for kids, and specials for taking private lessons. He's pulled all of his advertising."

I bit my lip as I considered Kenneth Simpson or really anyone who was affected by the higher advertising cost as a possible suspect. If Horace wasn't at the station anymore, Vick would be forced to lower his advertising dollars, since he believed the airtime warranted such high advertising costs.

"I've got to go. There can't be much time left before I have to play another set of songs." She lifted the bakery bag in the air. "Thanks for the cookies. I'll be at the wedding. After all, everything here is recorded. So if Levi didn't do it, I guess he'll be at your wedding too."

"Is he here?" It would be simple enough to ask him now, though I still had to finish my second loop of deliveries and pick up the third loop.

"Nope. He really doesn't have a set schedule anymore." She stopped at the door of the radio station and turned around. "See, he's the perfect suspect."

The perfect suspect. I wanted to blurt out, "He and all the advertisers who have gotten hit with the cost of Horace LeLand," but I didn't.

Lucy Drake's account of what was going on behind the scenes at WSCG was definitely fishy.

The bell over Tabor Architects dinged announcing my arrival. The front office where Julia's desk was located was empty, but the light was on in Mac's office.

"Mac? Julia?" I called out and dug down in my bag for his office mail. I hadn't planned on stopping in today and would have completely walked past the office on my way to talk to Lucy. Now that I couldn't help but wonder if Levi killed Horace, though, our wedding entertainment could be in jeopardy.

The number of DJs around here had dropped to virtually zero if that was the case.

"This is a happy surprise." Mac came out of his office, looking at his watch. "I thought we were meeting for lunch?"

"We are, but I had to stop in because I just got some disturbing news." I heard the bathroom sink turn on and some shuffling in there before Julia emerged. "Hey there." My voice grew. "I'm so happy to see you."

I gave her a big hug.

"Mac said y'all were having lunch. Is it already lunchtime?" A sudden look of urgency appeared in Julia's eyes.

Her blond hair was pulled back in a low ponytail, something she'd been wearing since Clara had found it funny to tug on anything she could get her little grip around.

"No. No." Mac waved his hands. "You've still got a couple of hours to get the proposal in."

"Goodness." She put her hands to her chest. "I thought I'd lost track of time." She smiled. "Mac told me about last night too. I called Grady, and he was pretty upset about it."

"Yeah. He called me and let me know. How's Clara this morning?" I asked.

"The whole gluten-free thing isn't working for us. She keeps crying for fishy crackers and won't stop." She snorted. "I actually called to see if your mom and dad wanted to pick her up from daycare early. It's my way of getting Clara to settle down."

"How's that?" I asked.

"They give her fishy crackers, even though they aren't gluten free, which means Clara will be a happy little girl tonight for Grady and me." Julia surprised me. "Honestly, it's Grady who thinks we should be all gluten free with the fertility issues and all, but the doctor said there was no research linking being gluten free and fertility."

"You have probably made my parents' day." I laughed. "But I told them they had to respect your wishes."

"But do they?" she asked in an entertaining tone.

"If that's the case"—I pulled out another little bag from Pie in the Face—"how about some freshly baked Pumpkin Sugar Cookies to take home?"

"Grady will give in for sure with these." Julia took them and set them on her desk. "Let him be the one to tell you about this whole crazy gluten thing. I'm shocked Mac hasn't let you in on my little lunches here."

"I did not. It's not my place. I can keep secrets." Mac

wasn't about to betray anyone's trust, and I loved his loyalty. He was one of the good ones.

"You two!" My jaw dropped. "You have to come clean about this. Everyone in town is on pins and needles about your decision."

"I'll talk to Grady and tell him I'm not going to keep Clara on the gluten-free track." Julia was going to make a lot of people happy. "I will just have to wait, pray, and hope we are blessed with another baby. If not, Clara is pretty darn perfect."

"I'm happy to hear you say that." It was comforting to hear Julia realize that sometimes what you wanted wasn't in the cards and to continue to see the blessing in what she had. "She is a blessing. Speaking of blessings"—I turned to Mac—"I'm here because of our wedding and how blessed we are to have found our love. And I'm not trying to worry too much about the day, but have you spoken to Levi?"

The phone in Mac's office started ringing. "Excuse me." Julia hurried back into the office. "That could be the construction manager. I don't want to miss his call."

"I haven't talked to him this week. Normally, I'll see him walking to work, but I've been too busy to notice. Why?" He reached out and took my hand. "What's with the look?"

"I was talking to Lucy, and she gave me a really good reason for him to be the killer," I whispered like someone was around to hear me.

"Levi?" Mac laughed like it was a joke. "Wait. You're serious." He dropped my hand.

"Yes. But don't mind that now. All I care about at this moment is if we will have a DJ or not for the reception." This was the one detail I'd left up to Mac to take care of. Everything else Iris or I did helped.

"I'll give him a call before I meet you for lunch." Julia called for Mac. "I have to get back to the proposal if we are going to have some food on the table this winter."

"We will be fine." I had all the faith in the world life would just get better and better once I was his wife. "We can live on love."

"That we have plenty of." He bent down and kissed my lips. "See you in a couple of hours."

I'd not told Mac about Kenneth Simpson or that more than just the country club had pulled advertising. Mac was preoccupied with getting the bid finished. He didn't have to tell me it was because he wanted everything buttoned up before we left on our honeymoon.

The thought of us going to a beach for a full week would sound like heaven if I didn't have this crazy murder looming over my head. It wasn't like I could just switch my thinking off now that I'd decided to snoop around and see just why Vince or Sandra was the target.

A couple of hours would be all I needed to deliver the third loop if I jumped in the LLV, which made me hurry back down the street to the post office. I knew the time would go fast with my head all jumbled up with possible new suspects. The list of advertisers could go on forever, which would take me more than the next few days to look into.

Good thing a lot of the advertisers were on my route, and I could pick their brains to see what they thought about the price increase or if they'd stuck with advertising on the radio. More importantly, I could see if it hurt their businesses' bottom line.

"You're early," Monica called back into the mail room when she noticed me coming in to grab the third-loop mail she'd already stacked for me.

"Yeah. I haven't had too many chit-chatty people today. I even took a pit stop at the bakery to chat with Iris," I told her and started to go through the box of mail. "There's a lot of mail here."

"There's a package for Kay Tedle in there. She called and said she'd seen it come through her daily delivery email. She told me to just give it to you because she said she was told you were going to the Elks Club or something." Monica shrugged and proceeded to help the next customer in line at the counter.

Customers really weren't supposed to ask us to do anything with their mail other than deliver it to the specified addresses, but it was different in Sugar Creek Gap. The town was small enough that we were able to take the few requests we'd gotten. And I didn't mind.

I was going there, like she said, and it wouldn't hurt to take this request.

I loaded up the box in the back of the LLV and was happy to see all the things on my checklist checked off so I could leave without any problems.

Instead of hitting the neighborhood, which took up the entire third loop and was the longest part of my shift, I drove out of downtown toward the Elks Lodge with one thing in mind.

Talking to Sandra Rothchester.

The Elks Lodge was a place for everyone. They had a men's club and a women's club. My mom and the Front Porch Ladies were members of the Elks Women's Club. They hosted several events like grab-a-date dances and holiday parties as well as a crafty women's day like today. Sara Rammond was bringing her talent into the floral department so they could make a fun fall wreath.

The Elks Club was essentially a steel-pole-barn-type dwelling with a few beers on tap in the back. The tap was next to the kitchen, where the staff heated up food people brought in for events.

Today was no different. When I walked in, I could smell the mixture of casseroles and dishes alongside platters of simple desserts like cookies and bars, all lined up on the banquet table in the back.

The round tables in the middle of the floor held dried

leaves, fake greenery, sticks of glue for the hot glue guns, and other embellishments to add to the grapevine wreaths.

"What do you think about this one?" Millie Barnes lifted two little plastic pumpkins. "I was thinking I could glue those right here."

Sara stood over her and made a couple of suggestions before Millie picked up the hot glue gun and shot some in the spot Sara suggested.

"These look great." I glanced around at the ladies, who suddenly realized I was there. "Here you go." I'd seen Kay right off next to my mom.

"That's what I call a good service," Kay teased. "Thank you, Bernie." She leaned over to Mom. "You sure do have a good one."

"I hear you get to pick up Clara early today." I sat down in the empty chair next to Mom and looked at her wreath. She'd picked a strand of the ivy garland to wrap around the grapevine wreath and a few orange silky leaves to go on each side of a small scarecrow embellishment. "And I hear you can give her these Pumpkin Sugar Cookies."

I had brought some in with Kay's package.

"Not if those are gluten free." Mom scoffed, rolling her eyes at the bag before she went back to manipulating the wire in the leaves to form them in the exact way she wanted.

"You and I both know you're going to give her fishy crackers." I tilted my head from side to side to get a look at her creation. "Besides, Julia isn't going to follow the gluten-free lifestyle anymore. The doctor told her there was no sense in them carrying on with it because nothing has come back to prove to them that's the reason they can't get pregnant."

"I knew it." It was like the life had been blown back into Mom. "Everyone told me the same thing."

"Don't even bring it up again. Julia doesn't need the 'I told you so,' and Grady will just ignore it too." Mom was good at making sure everyone knew she was right all along, and it didn't go well when Grady had as big a head as she did.

"I won't." She shrugged and put the wreath down on the table. "Are those freshly baked?"

"Yes." I smiled and ran my finger along her wreath. "This is really good, Mom."

"Thank you, honey." She picked it up and looked at it one more time. "I think I'll make another one so I can put them on the front door of the diner. Our fall menu will start this weekend with chili for the big game."

"Big weekend for you." Sara Rammond walked up when she noticed I'd sat down. "You are going to love the flowers Larry insists on having on the tables for your big day."

She pulled her phone from the pocket of her apron and tapped the screen a few times before turning the phone around to show me the photos.

"He insisted on this garland-style spray." The photo she was showing me was nothing I'd ever seen. It certainly was not at all what I expected my second wedding to even look like.

"He has used the dahlia as the main flower, accented with avalanche rose, Vendela rose, rosebud, fluffy mini pampas grass, and amber eucalyptus leaves. Something about creating a unique and rustic wedding dinner table for the awesome couple." Her words even sounded pretty as she spouted off the flowers' names while pointing at the respective images.

"I don't have any words." The images were so gorgeous my eyes welled. "They are." I gulped back the lump forming in my throat. "Amazing," I whispered and felt her and my mom put a hand on me.

"You deserve amazing. You deserve gorgeous. You deserve so much more." Sara's words touched my heart. "You are going to be so happy, and we are so grateful you're letting Leaf and Petal be part of it."

"I'm honored you even said yes. If they are this gorgeous in photos, I can't imagine what they will look like in person." I couldn't take my eyes off her phone. This was the first time I'd even pictured what the day would look like. I'd been so busy trying to figure out who killed Horace and attempted to kill Vince, but now that I'd seen the photos of the flowers, the images of my wedding day were starting to pop into my head.

My heart swelled.

"Speaking of the big day..." I knew I had to shift to why I'd come so I could get to my lunch with Mac on time. "I was wondering if I could speak to you?"

"Is something wrong?" Mom asked, her frown lines creasing.

"No. Nothing like that." I laid to rest the idea that anything was wrong with the wedding and got up to follow Sara over to the little bar the Elks kept in the back for the men.

"Is everything okay with the flowers?" I detected a gnawing at Sara's confidence.

"They are great," I gushed. "I know I should be focusing on the wedding, but my problem is Vince and his safety. I'm sure you heard about Horace LeLand." She nodded. "He was killed with a letter opener to the brain. Like someone did to Vince. I was resistant to Vince's theory he was stabbed, since it just didn't make sense that someone would want to kill him. Without going into detail, I've traced a line between Vince and Horace. Millie told me Sandra, Horace's mother-in-law, did the wreath class and stayed after sometimes for you to help her because of her arthritis." I took another look around the room to see if I'd missed seeing Sandra. "I was going to ask her a few questions and noticed she's not here. Which I'm sure is because of what happened to Horace last night."

"I'm sure that's it." Sara blinked a few times. "But I'm not sure how I can help."

"I'm looking for anything. Did she ever mention Melissa and Horace having problems?" I asked.

"She never said it directly, but I think she felt like a burden to them." My mind took hold of the word "burden."

Wanting to get rid of a burden would be a good reason for Horace to have tried to kill Sandra, like my newest theory had laid out. Melissa would have an excellent motive to have killed Horace if she'd put two and two together.

"I also know he and Melissa had some sort of arrangement for payment for Sandra so she didn't live in their home. I'm not sure what it was, and don't hold me to it, but I do remember her saying something when we were alone after class working on the bow of her wreath. She'd gotten a call from Horace. He was upset she'd used the salon a couple of times in a month. Vivian adds salon use on to your monthly bill. Then he mentioned a steak dinner for two and…" She stopped talking, drew in her brows, and pressed her lips together. "Something about Vince Caldwell."

"Vince?" I asked, not remembering Vince even mentioning anything about Sandra or a steak dinner.

"I'm sorry to be the one to even tell you this because I know you and Vince are tight, but Sandra told me they are dating." Sara looked down at her phone and then put it back in her apron.

"Wait." I blinked and quickly shook my head a couple of times. "What?"

"They are an item, and if what you are saying is true about the tie between Vince and Horace, do you think someone is going to hurt Sandra?" Sara asked a great question I'd been toying with, only on my end I was thinking Vince was mistaken. Now I wasn't so sure. Someone might want anyone who might come between Sandra and Melissa dead.

The only someone who would be threatened was Melissa LeLand.

But why?

Chapter 10

"You look hurt." Mac shoved a big spoonful of macaroni and cheese in his mouth.

"I am hurt. Vince is dating Sandra, and someone tried to kill him. He left that out?" I was leaning over on my forearms and whispering across the table at the Wallflower Diner just in case someone was trying to listen in. "His girlfriend's son-in-law is murdered, and he didn't think to have any reason to tell me, since that's the tie I'm following to help him figure out who tried to kill him."

"I don't know, Bernie. I guess you'll have to ask him flat out." He dug the spoon back in the small crock Mom used to pack the single-serve gooey, cheesy deliciousness in when she put it in the oven. The crock created the little bit of brown crust with parmesan cheese when placed in the oven's heat. "I do know we need to talk about our living arrangements."

"I know." I pushed back from the table and wiggled around in the vinyl seat to get comfy before I dug into my BLT, another favorite with the customers. I picked up the top piece of toast and slathered more of the mayonnaise across it before I replaced it.

I took a big bite.

"What are you thinking?" I asked through a mouthful of food but covered my mouth up with my napkin for some semblance of good manners.

"I know my house is bigger, but your house is homier, and Clara knows your house." He was so sweet to even think about her comfort. "I wouldn't want her to have to get used to staying somewhere new. Plus, the animals are at home."

"Mac Tabor, I couldn't love you any more than I do right this minute." For the second time today, my eyes welled with tears. "I don't know why I'm so weepy today." I used the edge of the napkin to dab the corner of my eyes. "Good thing Mom is still at the Elks', or she'd be rushing over to see why I'm crying."

"I guess I just want you to finally be happy. It's the only thing I've ever wanted for you since the day I met you. Then when you and Richard had Grady, I only wanted the best for you and Grady. Now I get to make sure you are happy. Before, I wasn't able to give you happiness." Gently he smiled.

My eyes clouded over from the tears.

He got up from his side of the booth, slid in next to me, and put his arm around me. I rested my head on his shoulder.

"It wasn't my place to give you happiness. Now I get to make you happy. It's a mission I've wanted for so long. You being happy gives me great joy, and I couldn't imagine not spending the rest of my life even thinking differently. That's why I want you not to have any stress over where we live and how you do things daily. A seamless transition, only you get to share a bed with Rowena and Buster and me." Cradling me more closely, he rubbed my arm, comforting me with not only his words but his embrace. "Don't you want that for Vince?"

I jerked my head off his shoulder.

"Was that entire speech for me to see Vince's point of view?" My tears dried up quickly.

Mac laughed.

"No. But if you took it that way, maybe it's a sign. I will tell you that I'm excited to move into your house. We can put mine on the market. Now back to Vince." He reached across the table and dragged his plate of food over to him. "Is it possible Sandra has it mixed up? Vince was kind to her, and she took it as him wanting to date her?"

"I never thought about it that way, but I guess it could be a possibility." I picked up my sandwich and took a bite. "But I do know Horace was upset Sandra had spent the money for her hair and this now-infamous steak dinner for Vince. That makes me think Sandra told Melissa about the call, and really there's no easy solution other than to ask Melissa herself."

"How are you going to do that? At this time?" Mac asked.

"I'm going to take her some cookies." I still had some from Iris and planned to drop them off for the repast. Also, the funeral home wasn't too far from my third loop, and I was in the LLV, so it wouldn't take that long to stop by. "Now back to the wedding. I tasted the cakes, and your red velvet is going to be a hit."

"Iris always knocks it out of the park." He wiggled his brows. "I can't wait to have a piece after you become my wife."

Then Mac said something that I'd never even considered.

"Mrs. Bernadette Tabor." The words rolled out of his mouth.

My mouth dried. Suddenly an echo formed around me, like I was in a tunnel and a different zone.

"I've been dying to call you that for so long, and now it's going to come true." He tilted his head and looked at me. "Bernadette Tabor. It has a nice ring to it."

My hand shook as I went to pick up the glass of iced tea and tried to wet my whistle.

"Are you feeling okay?" he asked.

I had to disguise my involuntary reaction to how he'd changed my name by giving him a gentle, loving look.

"Yeah. Just a little tired." I held the glass between both hands to stop the shaking. "That's all."

Over the course of the rest of lunch, I brought up everything under the sun to change the subject.

My mind was split down the middle with two separate thoughts, and I was getting a headache thinking about them.

There was no good way to tell Mac I'd not even considered changing my name to his, so instead of worrying about that, I decided to make a pit stop after my third loop. I would go to the funeral home to see if the layout time for Horace LeLand had been planned or where Baron Long planned to release his body.

"Did you happen to get in touch with Levi?" I asked.

"I left him a message, so I'm hoping he'll call back soon." Mac touched my leg. I glanced up, feeling an odd sensation traveling through me from his touch. "I want you to be careful. I know you're trying to really figure out Horace's murder and why someone would hurt Vince, and you know I don't care if you gossip here and there, but I do want you to be safe. Sheriff Hafley hasn't brought anyone in for questioning, which tells me they don't have a good suspect."

"Maybe she's not looking at all possibilities." I picked up my glass and took a drink. "It could be anyone. Even Dad." I threw my dad a look.

He was behind the counter while Mom was still at the Elks' making her wreath.

"Your dad?" Mac wrinkled his nose in confusion.

"Not really but a business owner." I glanced around to make sure no one was within earshot of me because I certainly didn't need it all over town that I was pointing fingers at innocent people for murder. "According to Lucy Drake, when Vick hired Horace LeLand, everyone's bonuses and airtime had been cut. Having your income cut really does mess with someone's livelihood, right?"

"Yeah. I'd guess that's right." Mac nodded, his eyes lowered.

"Lucy said the advertising also tripled. Now I know my parents don't advertise the diner, but I do know a lot of businesses around here do. They rely on the advertising to bring in customers but not at the higher cost."

"Vick stopped by the office the week he hired Horace. He was bragging about how the station was going to go up in rank with Horace joining." The corner of Mac's lip ticked up as he recalled the memory. "He gave me a price sheet for advertising, saying they'd just completed their quarterly review, and they did raise their advertising, but the return was going to be at least double if not triple because of Horace joining the team."

"He did?" I knew I had to talk to Vick Morris about advertisers who'd pulled their ads or even complained.

"Yeah. I told him I was a one-man show, and though it sounded like a winning strategy, I wouldn't even be able to take on new clients, but I'd let him know." Mac didn't need to spend any money to promote Tabor Architects. Everyone in town already knew him, and word of mouth was his greatest source of advertising. He didn't need the radio.

"You are the best." I fluttered my lashes. "Especially with everyone in town wanting to remodel. You're the best with those." I grabbed his chin with my fingers and gave him a peck. "You have a brilliant mind when it comes to what walls need to be knocked down or built up."

"And if I want to get my plate cleared for our honeymoon, I've got to get back to work." He pulled his wallet out of his pants pocket and put some money on the table to cover the tab, though Dad would be so mad.

My parents never wanted us to pay to eat there. They

claimed it was no different than them having us over for supper. Like advertising, though, they didn't do it for free.

Vick Morris certainly wasn't giving anyone free advertising.

"I'll see you later." Mac and I gave each other one more goodbye hug and kiss before he took a left out of the diner to go back to the office. I jumped in the LLV parked in front of the diner.

As the LLV rattled down Main Street toward the neighborhood for the third loop, it was hard not to notice the fall banners the Beautification Committee had hung off the posts of the carriage lights. I was impressed with how they'd incorporated the image of a football intwined with the fall leaf design, showcasing the two things the residents of Sugar Creek Gap loved most about the fall.

The woods surrounding our little town in the hollow were starting to turn brilliant shades of orange, yellow, and red mixed in with varying colors of green. As the bright sun hung high in the sky, it raised the autumn temperature just enough for me to have to peel off my sweatshirt.

The Sugar Creek Gap Golf Course lay on the right, and no matter how hard I tried to keep driving past it, telling myself I had to get the third loop delivered, I sure didn't listen.

It was like my foot and my hands took over, swinging the LLV into the entrance of the golf course. My eyes took in the one hundred twenty-seven acres of golf course, restaurant, and pool. I knew it took a lot to run the place. Advertising was a big deal to them, and well, if they used WSCG like they used to, then they had a say in the higher cost of taking out a thirty-second ad.

Too bad I didn't have the country-club neighborhood on my route. I'd be able to kill two birds with one stone, I thought as I drove past the expensive homes. Their homeowner's fee was more than a monthly house payment, which gave an advertiser another reason to be so mad that they'd do just about anything to keep the country club running.

It wasn't too long ago when the country club almost went under because of the price of staying open. They would stop short of nothing to keep the country club going, and it was a huge debate at many town council meetings. If I recalled correctly Kenneth Simpson was even at the forefront of that murder investigation.

Luckily, it turned out Kenneth had nothing to do with it, but that didn't mean he was innocent of what had happened to Horace.

There was a small putt-putt golf area outside of the clubhouse closest to the first tee. Though families could use the area to play putt-putt, most golfers used it to work on their putt before starting a golf game.

"Don't these men work?" I asked when I got out of the LLV and noticed just how many cars were in the parking lot. Furthermore, the golf carts that were usually lined up underneath the garage awning were all gone.

It dawned on me that I should've called ahead to see if Kenneth was even available, but I took my chance and headed into the pro shop where his office was located.

"Hey, Bernie!" Kenneth and a couple of other men were standing next to a cardboard box. "What about giving Mac one of these as a wedding gift?" He picked up a shirt from the box and held it up. "It's got the new logo on it."

"The country club has a new logo?" I asked.

"Yeah. Thanks to Mac. He designed it." This was yet another previously unknown project of Mac's, and I had no idea what he had done. "Pretty great."

"You should be giving him one." I shrugged.

The men snickered.

"Yeah. With the price it cost me to hire him, he could buy

one." Kenneth tossed the shirt back into the box. "Are you filling in today?"

That was a standard question I got when I was on someone else's route instead of my own.

"Actually, I wanted to talk to you." I looked between the two men standing with Kenneth. "Do you have a minute?"

"I sure do." He tilted his head, indicating for me to follow him. "You hungry? Can I buy you lunch?"

We headed outside, where the buzz of golf carts whirled by, the sound of golf clubs smacking golf balls echoed, and the chatter of laughter from players and the hint of a cigar smell floated past us.

"Thank you. I've already eaten." I sucked in a deep breath and let go of a heavy sigh. "My friend Vince Caldwell had that accident a few months ago."

"Yeah. I heard about that. At first, they thought he wasn't going to make it." Kenneth brought back the painful memory. "Emmalynn told me he was back home."

"How is Emmalynn?" I had lost my manners and should've asked about his wife before I even thought about bringing up the murder.

"She's great. She's desperately trying to get Teri home now that she's graduated, but Teri doesn't want to come back." The lines around his mouth pulled as he frowned.

"I can't believe she's already graduated from college." Life was passing by so fast. "It seemed like yesterday she was on the field cheering."

"Speaking of cheering, how's Grady feeling about the big game this week?" He had just asked the million-dollar question.

"I don't ask. I just keep my mouth shut. Thank you for the donation, by the way." I knew the booster committee had already sent the thank-you notes, but this was a great opportunity to go right into my questions about the advertising situation.

"This is the first time someone from the booster club stopped by to personally thank us." Kenneth pretended to know why I was there, and by his tone, I knew he was kidding.

"I do have the big broadcast sponsorship, if you're interested." I had no reason to avoid trying to sell that while I was here. "With WSCG's cutbacks, they didn't keep the broadcast this year, and I'm just finding out about it."

"That means the country club would have to give Vick the money for them to broadcast it, and I'm not giving Vick Morris a dime after what he pulled." Kenneth spat with disgust. "That man truly thinks he can hire whoever he wants and triple advertising costs in a small town like Sugar Creek Gap. He can take his radio and shove it up—" He tucked his lips in tight. "I'm not going to say where in front of a lady, so I'm going to politely decline."

"I had no idea you were so upset with them. I guess since you're their biggest advertiser, I didn't know anything was wrong," I lied, playing dumb.

"I pulled all my advertising after he raised the prices. It was robbery. Don't get me wrong. Horace LeLand was a big name in other markets, but when Vick brought him here, he didn't take into consideration that we are Sugar Creek Gap, a small town where we don't care about big numbers." He tapped his finger to his heart. "We care about people."

"Did you hear Horace was killed?" I asked.

"Sure did. Now I suspect Vick might go back to the way things were. Or he should because I don't recall ever hearing over the past few months any sort of increase in rank for the radio station. And what does that get WSCG anyways?" He asked so many good questions only one person would be able to answer.

Vick Morris himself.

"Where were you when Horace was killed?" I just threw it out there.

"Are you accusing me of something?" Kenneth's brows pinched. "This isn't the first time you've done that."

"I'm just asking, that's all." I played it off. "It's like, 'Where were you when you heard Elvis died?'"

"I was right here giving golf lessons. Now that we have the lights on the practice tees because of the extra money we found, since we aren't advertising, I'm able to give later night classes for kids who are busy after school or even people who can't make it during work hours." Kenneth smiled. "I guess I have Horace LeLand to thank for that."

"Yeah. That's a good way to look at it." I could tell by Kenneth's answer he wasn't lying. "So, I can count on you to sponsor the football game broadcasts?"

"I'll think about it." He smiled. "How about one of those golf shirts?"

"I'll take three. One each for Mac, Grady, and my dad." I knew I had to give a little if I wanted him to help with the boosters, and I knew that even more now that he told me how he'd been able to increase business with the new lights. The golf shirts would make great little thank-you gifts for the wedding.

I tucked the bag of shirts in the LLV once I got back in, satisfied with being able to mark Kenneth off my list of suspects, even though the little snooping stop had really set me back on my route.

The school traffic was heavy when I passed Sugar Creek Gap High on my way to the neighborhood where I ended my workday.

Instead of fighting the high school traffic by trying to deliver to the mailboxes and avoiding the vehicles, I pulled the LLV over to the side so I could give the kids a few minutes to get home from school and safely park in their driveways. I grabbed my phone to see if I had any text messages.

There was a missed call from Iris.

She answered the phone. "I've tried calling you twice. Where are you?"

"Pulled over to let the school traffic go before me. These kids will kill you, they drive so fast." I looked out at the side mirror and cringed. A student driver had gotten a little too snug to the LLV for me, nearly knocking off the mirror. "I swear they need to do a better road test down at the courthouse."

"You're getting grouchy in your old age," Iris teased.

"I'm following you," I joked back. "What's up?"

"I was going to tell you I got my first order for Horace's repass. His layout is going to be this weekend."

"You mean as in during my wedding?" I groaned, knowing funerals were a big deal to Iris's bottom line, and I couldn't ask her not to do it because she was doing my wedding stuff for free as a gift.

"Exactly." She confirmed what I didn't want to hear. "Don't worry. I'll have the order there before then. Or you will."

"Me?" I wondered what was up her sleeve.

"I got a call from Melissa LeLand. She asked if I could drop off some cookies tonight at the funeral home. She said they were going to go there tonight for the final preparation and sign off on the paperwork. Apparently, Angela Hafley has signed off to release the body to the family." Iris was full of useful information. "And there's no better time for you to over-hear some things."

"Jigs will go over the autopsy with them, and I'm curious to see how Melissa will react." I gnawed on the inside of my lip. "What time?"

"Six." It would be pretty much after I got off work, and I

really wanted to go back and see Vince to clarify a few matters. "Do you want to do it?"

"Yes, I'm going to do it." I thought about the rest of my day. "I think Vince is hiding something."

"Vince? Really?" Iris's lack of shock surprised me.

"You knew he was seeing Sandra, don't you?" I knew it.

"I didn't know. I had my suspicions up until his accident. Do you remember the night you couldn't make bingo because you were babysitting Clara when Julia came up with the summer cold?"

"Yes." There were a few times I hadn't helped Iris at the senior living facility during bingo.

"That night, they came in together. The rumors were flying about how he'd moved into the main facility to be closer to her and how she'd gotten her claws into him. Those old ladies can be mean." Iris snickered. "Slim pickings."

"Why didn't you say anything?" I asked.

"I remember calling you to check up on Melissa, and you were talking about Clara, so I totally forgot about it. Then he had his accident. Even when you brought up the connection between Horace and Vince, I didn't remember."

"What sparked your memory?" I asked.

"Today, when Melissa called about tonight's order, I over-heard Sandra in the background saying something about 'Vince's favorite' or 'order Vince's favorite.' I asked Melissa what her mom was saying, and she pooh-poohed it," Iris recalled.

"Pooh-poohed it?" I asked, seeking more clarification.

"Yeah, like she didn't even want to go there or visit the subject. Kinda had a tone of being put off or something." Iris's words made it even more urgent for me to see Melissa LeLand in person.

"We will definitely get to the bottom of this." I put the LLV in gear and hit the gas. If I was going to finish by six, I had to get going on the rest of the deliveries, crazy high school kid drivers or not.

"We?" Iris chuckled.

"Yes. You and me. I'll pick you up at six." I hung up the phone, and by the time I got all the mail delivered, I had enough time to hurry home, feed Rowena, let Buster out, feed him, and change my clothes before I got into my car to pick up Iris.

"Are you ready?" I walked into the bakery to help her carry some of the bakery boxes for the repast to the car.

"Back here!" Iris called from the back. "Come on back."

When I pushed through the kitchen door, I saw Iris wasn't alone.

Vince Caldwell, Sandra Rothchester, and Melissa LeLand were with her.

Chapter 11

"Melissa, I'm so sorry to hear about Horace." I immediately greeted Melissa once my head had wrapped around the sight of the three of them standing there.

My gaze slid over to the wipe-off board, where Vince was standing with his legs slightly apart, his arms crossed, and his eyes focused on what Iris and I had written on there.

"Thank you. We are just devastated, and I was telling Iris how grateful I am she's able to get the desserts made so quickly with your wedding and all." Melissa gave me a sympathetic smile.

"She is a gem," I said and gave Iris a glance. "I'm sorry I won't be able to attend the funeral Saturday. I'm getting married."

"Gosh." Vince twisted around. "I forgot about that."

My eyes shot up with one question in my mind. How did he forget? We'd been talking about this for months.

"Sandra, I will have to go to Bernie's wedding." He walked over to Sandra, and I noticed he was getting stronger with each passing day. "She's almost like a daughter to me."

"Can I see you for a minute?" I directed my question to

Vince, though I didn't state it so much as a question but as a request. I expected him to follow me out the kitchen door, so I didn't wait for him to answer before I left the kitchen.

"Why didn't you tell me you were seeing Sandra?" I asked him as soon as he emerged. "I guess the little fact escaped your memory?"

"I was busy trying to get better and figure out who had tried to kill me over the last few months." As he spoke, I gave him a good look and noticed his coloring was almost all back to normal. "Getting better was what I was focusing on, but yeah, we've had a couple of dates here and there."

"You didn't think to let me in on that because I have good motive to believe Melissa killed Horace, and Horace tried to kill Sandra. All over money." I sighed.

"That's where you're wrong." Vince had a determined look on his face. "If you'll come back into the kitchen and let me explain why we three are here together, then I think you'll see Melissa and Sandra are not suspects."

"Fine." I headed back into the kitchen, my interest piqued over why Vince didn't believe my theory about Melissa's very good motive to have had killed her husband.

Iris, Melissa, and Sandra were standing in front of the wipe-off board when Vince and I went to rejoin them.

"I can't believe you think I killed my husband." Melissa had an expression indicating she thought it was the most outrageous theory anyone could have. "Or that my mother would be part of the reason he's dead."

"Let me explain." I knew Vince had something to say about this matter, too, but I wanted my reason for coming up with this theory to be on the record. "I believe someone thought Vince was your mom, since your mom had been staying in that room while she waited for her more permanent room." I smiled at Sandra and received a grin in return. "When I overheard you, your mom, and Horace arguing over the payment for her room the other day before bingo, I couldn't help but believe a motive for Horace to have attempted to kill you"—I directed this part of the explanation of my theory to Sandra—"was the money he was paying out for you to stay there."

"The money? Horace had money?" Melissa threw her head back and cackled. "He didn't have any money but the money she gave him so she could outwit Medicare."

"Excuse me?" Her statement baffled and confused me.

"When you sign up to live in a senior living facility, you give them access to your records, including your money." Sandra put a hand on her daughter's arm. "I didn't ever want to be a burden on my family, and there's nothing wrong with me, like Vince. We live there because of the wonderful community and no burden to our children. If we are lucky, we get to meet someone like you there along the way."

Sandra's head swiveled. She gestured to Vince.

"Vince loves you like a daughter. He told me all about you and your life." As she spoke about him, he walked over and put an arm around her. "We have found a common bond that's brought us great companionship." She placed a palm on his chest.

"Mom has a lot of money. We just couldn't sign over her accounts to the senior living facility, so we found a loophole in the system." Melissa began telling what they'd been doing. "You see, if Mom loaned all of her money to Horace and me, then she doesn't have any money for the senior living facility to take, so they start using the Medicare. We were able to take all of Mom's money and have her sign papers over to loan all her money to us. We don't touch the money. Every month, Horace writes Mom a loan payment out of the money she loaned us, and that payment goes to Vivian for Mom's extra things outside of what the actual cost of living there is. So when I asked Horace if he paid, I wanted to make sure nothing got snafued."

"Is all of that legal?" I asked, since I'd never heard of such a thing.

"Completely," Melissa confirmed. "But it doesn't mean Horace and I were happy. We weren't. The problem is the loan is in both of our names. If I were to divorce him, he told me he'd not let me assume the loan, tying my hands to him."

"That gives you even more motive than I thought of before," I said, stating the obvious but not to her liking. "Let me explain," I added, stopping her from talking. "If someone on the loan dies, the other will just automatically absorb the loan. If you weren't happy in your marriage, it would come out, and then this loan stuff would also come to light."

"I didn't kill him. I knew Sheriff Hafley was getting at something." Melissa bit her lip as though she were holding something back. Her nostril flared. "Leave it to Horace to have the last laugh."

"You need to tell her. Vince said she can be trusted." Sandra encouraged her daughter to tell me what she was talking about.

"You can trust both of these ladies." Vince pointed between Iris and me. "They have a way of getting to the bottom of things. People in this town trust them."

"Horace and I had an agreement years ago. He's always had a wandering eye, and I don't care. The only thing I cared about was my mom." Melissa gave her mom a frown. "Horace's job has taken us all over the world, and I love that. I had to give a little in order to travel with him, and that meant letting him have an open marriage."

"You mean to tell me you encouraged him to cheat on you?" Iris choked. She grabbed a cookie and stuffed it in her mouth. "This is the kind of stuff that happens in movies, not here in Sugar Creek Gap."

"I know it sounds terrible." The edges of Sandra's eyes turned down. "Please don't judge my daughter for it. She's been trying to get out of the marriage, but Horace wouldn't."

"Again, another motive for Melissa to be Angela Hafley's number-one suspect." I hated to give them the little bit of news, but the issue was as clear as day. "Melissa wanted her life without Horace, and she made sure of it."

"What would have happened to the loan if Sandra was killed?" Iris asked.

"It would've been forgiven. There's a clause in the loan papers the lawyer made up stating if something happened to Mom, then we didn't have to pay the loan." Melissa shook her head. "When Vince told us today about the theory that someone mistook him for my mom, I couldn't help but think Horace might've tried to kill her because he was starting to come around about a divorce. If Mom was dead and we got the loan money, then he could divorce me and take half."

"What do you mean he was coming around to thinking about a divorce?" I asked. "What changed?"

"Tracey Damski." Melissa snorted.

"You mean Tracey Damski as in DJ Damski? The Sunday-afternoon DJ?" Iris knew much more about who was employed and who wasn't at the WSCG station because she always had the radio on when she baked. "I listen to her every Sunday while I'm in here baking for the upcoming week."

"Yes. Horace had his eye on her from the first day he took the position at the radio station. They hit it off right away. I could see it from the moment they laid eyes on each other when Vick Morris introduced us at the welcome party the station threw." Melissa huffed a snort and then rolled her eyes. "I told Horace as soon as we got home, and he made fun of me for even thinking such a thing, as though it didn't happen at each station along the way."

"What happened?" Iris's curiosity was her greatest vice,

and I loved it. She never held back from asking the yucky questions when it came to deeply personal stuff. I always seemed to dance around them.

"She happened. I was right. They'd been secretly seeing each other, although he tried to tell me they weren't and he was on the up and up." A sadness shone in her eyes as she retold the story. "Now that Vince brought up how Horace could've killed Mom, I have to believe it was because of the affair with Tracey. I found this."

Melissa dug down into her purse and pulled out a piece of paper, which she handed to me.

Iris stood behind me, looking at the piece of paper.

"That's an email from Tracey to Horace. It came to our personal email, not our work email, so it wouldn't be seen by anyone but Horace. He had a strict policy with his women friends not to communicate during work hours, on work phones, or any devices, including email. As you can see at the top, it's his home personal email. She writes how she cannot be the other woman, and if he wanted to have a chance he had to be single." She talked with a crisp, to-the-point tone. "That means a clear path would be to kill Mom, divorce me, and take half so he could have somewhat of a decent life. The radio station can't afford to keep him here after his contract is up in a few months."

"A few months? You just got here." Iris was good at catching details. She stuffed another cookie in her mouth as she walked over to the wipe-off board.

She left Melissa's name as a suspect but added Tracey Damski as another.

While Melissa continued to give the details about Horace and Tracey Damski, Iris wrote them down.

"Now for the salary. Horace has always had a big ego. He has that personality where everyone who meets him loves him. His viewers and listeners were the same. No matter if he gave a weather report that wasn't a bit accurate, he was able to do it in a way that reached his audience to create these super fans." She gave off a hint of satisfaction with a gleam in her eye. "It was very interesting to see. That made him very sought-after and marketable. With that comes big money. When you go to a small market where the viewership is less than stellar, cuts and changes have to be made in order to pay the hired help to come in and fix it."

"That's what Vick did." I recalled talking to Lucy Drake. "And that's why Levi and Tracey's hours were cut. Right?"

"Yes. From what I gather, Levi Horn was very upset because he was in line to be the new meteorologist." Melissa put her jazz hands in the air. "Surprise. Not only are you not getting the full-time gig, but you're being demoted to recorded weather reports. Good luck," she said, her voice cracking.

"Are you saying Levi Horn has a motive?" I asked to be clear.

"Now that you say it, he sure does. Him and Tracey Damski." After Melissa confirmed the details one more time, Iris and I had added two more people to our suspect list.

"How do we know you're not leading us on some goose chase?" I asked Melissa point-blank.

"I love my mom. I had no reason to divorce Horace or kill him. I am able to live my life and help my mom live her life. Horace was welcome to do whatever it was he wanted, and I guess I became too much baggage for his travels." Her brow winged up. "Besides, I was with Mom and Vince. After bingo, we got takeout for dinner and sat in Mom's room making Vince do his physical therapy exercises."

I looked at Vince, wanting him to not only confirm that he was doing his exercises but also agree to Melissa's alibi.

"Don't look so surprised." He gave me a hard look. "After you told me your theory, I knew I had to get the girls to tell you the truth. I already called Angela and told her they were with me. Even the log at the desk of the facility will show you the time Melissa signed in. You'll notice she didn't sign out because once she got the call from Vick about Horace, she left the facility in a hurry."

"You were there when Vick called?" I asked to make sure I heard him correctly.

"Yes," he confirmed with a firmness in his tone. "Melissa LeLand did not kill Horace. As far as Horace attempting to kill Sandra and mistaking me for her, I can't be sure of, and now that he's dead, I'm afraid we might not ever get the answer."

"If Tracey and Horace were as close as you believed them to be, she just might have the answer to that question." I sucked in a deep breath as the realization of the increasing complexity of the details of this case settled in my bones. "Now I'm worried I won't have all of this solved by the time I get my wedding dress on."

"What is the rush?" Melissa asked. "Why don't you tell Sheriff Hafley and let her take it from here?"

"Because I hired Levi Horn to do the music for my wedding, and Angela has a way of figuring out crimes when a big thing like a wedding or funeral is planned. I've come all this way not to have my wedding ruined." I pictured Angela storming to the farm on my wedding day to arrest Levi Horn. That wasn't how I wanted my little bit of sunshine in the social section of the newspaper to read.

"Then it looks like we are going to be really busy the next couple of days." Iris vigorously started to outline a timeline from the day Horace LeLand set foot in Sugar Creek Gap up to the time I was supposed to say "I do."

"This shouldn't be so hard. We only have two people to talk to." Iris stated it like nothing else in the world was going on between now and Saturday.

"Where are we going to fit it in with Clara's birthday and the football game?" I really was asking myself that as I looked at the whiteboard, trying to come up with any free time when there seemed to be none. "We are running out of time."

"Bernadette Butler, I told these ladies we could count on you." Vince wasn't going to let my apprehensiveness grow roots. "Now you do what you do best and what I've taught you over the years."

With the little confidence boost Vince gave me, I knew I had to see Tracey Damski first. A scorned lover seemed like a fitting place to start.

Chapter 12

"Breathe in." Peaches Partin could do all her yoga moves with her eyes closed and balance at the same time. "Breathe out." Her voice soothed even the most nervous Nelly of souls. "If you'd like to enjoy this pre-nuptial yoga as we celebrate our dear friend Bernadette Butler, close your eyes and listen to my voice as I guide you through this meditative offering."

"If I keep my eyes closed, I'll get dizzy and fall over." Iris didn't mean to be funny, but she caused everyone to snicker.

Ahem. Peaches cleared her throat.

The one leg I was standing on started to wiggle, since I'd lost focus while I peeked one eye open to look at Iris.

"Whoa." My arms whirled around to try to keep me balanced, like a flamingo's wings. "Dang." I fell to the ground and started to laugh, sending the rest of the group into a fit of laughter.

Rowena took the tumble as a way for her to come over and get some scratches along her back.

She and Buster knew the farm so well. Rowena had lived here with me, but Buster didn't. He'd lived in the house on Little Creek Road with the previous owner, a customer of mine, who left me the house in his will. Getting the house also meant taking care of Buster.

"You'll be a funny-looking bride with a cast on your leg or worse." Harriette Pearl patted her hip. "Your hips."

"Breathe in the gratitude for our friend Bernie!" Peaches took her job seriously, and by the tone of her voice, she was talking herself into her breathing in gratitude. "Breathe out the love for her upcoming union."

"Mamaw!" Clara didn't give two iotas about yoga. "No nap!" she screamed from the old wooden chair swing, which was attached to a low-hanging limb of the tree a few feet away from us. Her legs flailed in the air, nearly hitting Buster in the head.

Buster liked it when Clara was around. He'd taken pride in sitting next to her or beneath her in hopes something edible would drop from her chubby little fingers.

"Shhhh." Melissa put her finger to her mouth to shush Clara. Clara flung her little legs out straight as a stick in front of her and started to scream more loudly.

"No! Mamaw." Her scream turned into a cry, which she knew would send me right over there to pick her up.

"What if we sit on our yoga mats and tell our friend Bernadette how much we love her." Peaches made a suggestion everyone could get involved in.

"I'm sorry." There was no way I would let sweet Clara sit in the swing when she wanted me. Or least faked that she wanted me. Once I picked her up, she wiggled her way to the ground and toddled over to the group of ladies to test out everyone's lap until she finally got to Mom's.

"Nacky?" Clara put her hand out to my mom. "Nacky, Nana."

"Shhhh. That's Nana's little secret." My mom wasn't fooling anyone. "Nacky" was how I said the word "candy" when I was a baby, and it was passed down to Grady. The pronunciation had become a universal word for "candy" in our family, and Clara naturally picked it up.

Julia shook her head.

"You can give her a piece—a piece," Julia emphasized, "a piece of candy."

"Your mommy said you can have some nacky." Mom scooped Clara into her arms, popped up, and headed straight to the house. Before she opened the back screen door to the kitchen, she turned around and said, "Why don't y'all all come in and eat before Iris serves the cake."

The mention of food was all it took for Millie, Gertrude, Ruby, Revonda Gail, Julia, and Peaches to scurry off the yoga mats Peaches had brought, leaving me there in the corpse pose.

My soul filled as their chatter fluttered out the open windows of the old farmhouse. Though my friends and I were together a lot, hearing them come together specifically to celebrate a second wedding at my age truly meant something to me.

The farm took on a whole different look each season, and fall was one of my favorites. Even though the grass would be brown soon, the trees had started to shed their leaves, making the path around the area where the wedding would happen its own colorful carpet for me to take my walk down to Mac.

When Mac asked me to marry him, and we'd decided to wait for autumn, fall had seemed so far away. We loved being outside during these next few months. Both of us loved to sit on our porches and patios, grill out, and even take a few nightly strolls with the fur babies.

This was where Richard and I had spent our entire married life, and it was also the home where I'd grown up and spent most of my life, so it was natural to begin my new chapter right here with Mac Tabor.

"Breathe in," I whispered. I lay in the corpse position, eyes closed, one hand on my belly, the other on my heart. Peaches had taught me to do this position when I'd become so stressed out I started taking her class to learn how to chill. "Breathe out."

The sound of a car approaching caused me to bounce up on my elbows.

Levi.

I jumped to my feet and waved to him.

"I'm glad you got my text." I greeted him on my way over to his car. "Are you okay?" I asked, noticing the dark circles under his eyes. Something you might see from someone who hadn't been sleeping, had something on their conscience, maybe murdered someone.

"I'm good." He tried to disguise the lie by nodding and giving a faint smile.

"Really? Are you?" I asked. "I mean, I heard about your co-worker."

"Isn't it awful?" Levi was tall and thin. He had short blond hair. If I had to guess, I'd say he was in his thirties. He wore a pair of blue jeans, a green button-down shirt half tucked in, and a pair of tennis shoes.

"Is it?" I asked just to see his response. He glanced at me before deciding to change the subject.

"What's going on here?" He pointed off in the distance at the yoga mats.

"My bridal party." I used the term loosely, since Julia was the only one standing up with me, and Grady was going to be standing with Mac. "Decided I needed a bridal shower filled with yoga and food."

"That's nice." He rocked back on his heels. "I've got limited time tonight. I'm sorry I've not been able to call Mac back, but when I've DJ'd weddings before, I've found it's the bride who I really need to talk to about the events of the wedding."

"This bride wants to make sure you keep it clean and

going. That's it." I gestured for him to follow me around the side yard to the back of the farm, where we thought it would be nice to set up along the field near the small creek. Grady and Mac had already had the tents delivered back there and set up a cute little altar Grady had made out of some sticks. Though it didn't look like much now, Sara and Larry were going to weave the same flowers from the tablescape arrangement into the altar to make everything cohesive.

"We were going to have the dancing part of the reception under that tent." I pointed at the tent on the right. "That one is going to be where everyone will be able to sit and eat. Mac hired a bartender. They will have one bar set up under each tent. I guess you need to tell me where you'd like to set up. Then I'll decide where to put the bar."

"I'm going to have a few strobe lights, and I think it'd be nice if your guests were dancing facing the stream. The lights will look great mirroring the water." He had a good view as he pointed out the various places he was talking about before his phone chimed, immediately taking his attention. "I've got to go. Don't worry. Everything is going to look great."

I hurried next to him, trying to keep up the pace as he double-timed it back across the field in the direction of his car.

"Now that Horace is no longer at the radio station, do you think you'll be back on air, not recorded?" I had little time to get the answers I really wanted from him. I couldn't give two hoots about what music he played or even where he set up his equipment. We certainly didn't need strobe lights.

He stopped dead in his tracks and looked down at me, his face still.

"I think a lot of things need to happen at the station." He appeared as if he wanted to say something but held back. "Horace was leaving anyways."

"Leaving?" I asked.

"Yeah. I'm guessing you know my forecasts had been

shrunk to those recordings, since you mentioned it, so I had to take another job in order to help pay my bills. No thanks to Horace." He scoffed, not appearing to be a bit sorry about what had happened to Horace. "The only thing I could find that was flexible enough in case Vick called me in on a whim to fill in was a cleaning position for one of those companies who clean office space." His shoulders bounced as he laughed. "As fate would have it—and maybe to stab me in the back a little more—I was assigned to clean the station."

In the background, I could hear all the ladies in the kitchen laughing and enjoying themselves.

Rowena had found a rubbing post on Levi's legs, snaking her body from one shin to the other.

"I was in there one Sunday night and caught Horace with Tracey Damski. They were…" He blushed.

"I know. Melissa told me." I let him off the hook, since he looked embarrassed enough.

"Yeah. Apparently, they had this whole agreement or something." He threw a hand in disgust. "I quickly excused myself from the room and went into the offices to collect trash. I was nervous about the whole catching them because I knew if he gave the word to Vick, he'd fire me."

"What word?" I was confused.

"If Horace told Vick to fire me, Vick would. Vick does— did—everything Horace told him. I guess he had to because he's the one who spent all our money to hire Horace. Horace knew it too. He walked around the station like he was the one in charge and writing all the checks." He snorted. "Really, he was, but when I was emptying his trash, I accidentally knocked into his desk. His computer came to life, and Zoom popped up."

I wasn't sure where Levi was going with this, but it sure did seem important.

"Horace had been interviewing for new jobs. Bigger

markets. I got curious and started to poke around. I got so wrapped up into all the places he'd been interviewing and learning he took a job in Texas that I didn't even hear Tracey come into the office." Was Levi saying what I thought he was saying?

"She jumped down my throat, asking me why I was on Horace's computer, and I told her I knew he had taken a job in Texas. I guess he hadn't let her know, and she kinda had a meltdown. She started to tell me things about how they'd planned to go away together after Sandra died so he didn't have to be tied to Melissa anymore. They were going to live on some money he was going to get from Sandra's death, and he was leaving the meteorology field for a life with her." It sounded like Levi was telling me about a book he'd read, not a real-life occurrence. It was so strange.

"When was this?" I asked, trying to put together a timeline of events.

"Gosh. A few months ago." In other words, this was before Vince had gotten stabbed, which made me wonder if Tracey Damski had...

"When was the new job he took in Texas going to happen?" I asked.

"That's another thing, Tracey never told Horace I found out about the job. The next week I was there, they were there. I guess they met there on Sunday. There was no one in the building on Sunday anymore, since Vick took away all the live broadcasts and replaced them with syndicated shows and recorded weather reports." He rolled his eyes. "It was a perfect place for them to be alone. Every single Sunday night, I went there to clean, and they were there, huddled into a studio doing what I don't know, but I'm sure you can use your imagination."

"Yeah, no thank you." My lip twitched at the thought.

"I overheard them having an argument, and she blurted out that she knew he was going to leave once he got the bonus fulfilled on his contract." Levi's story was definitely pointing me in the direction of Tracey Damski, just like Melissa had mentioned.

"They had this big argument where he told her things had changed between him and Melissa. They were working things out, and he knew this new life in Texas would make them come together like man and wife as they should. Tracey smacked him across the face and said she'd done things for him no one would do."

"Things like try to kill Sandra a few months ago so they could be together." My thoughts ended up coming out of my mouth.

"What?" Levi squinted. "Tracey tried to kill Sandra?"

"No. I'm—umm." I pulled my lips tight and blinked a few times before tilting my head at him while collecting my thoughts. "No. Not that I know of. I have no idea why I would say that. I'm sorry. Go on."

"All I know is they broke up, and when I was cleaning the other night, I found him dead. On a Sunday. You do the math."

"You found him?" I realized I'd not known who had actually found him.

"Yeah. I thought it was strange because the door was unlocked. Every Sunday, when I went to clean, the doors were all locked up, but Horace and Tracey were inside. This time the door was unlocked. It made me stop, but I figured they'd gotten lax about meeting up in there, so I went on in and started my normal cleaning routine. When I got to the broadcast booth, that's when I found him." Levi looked off into the distance. His phone chirped again. "Sorry. I've got to go. It's Vick. I'm meeting him at the Wallflower Diner. I think he might be offering me a job, but joke's on him."

"What do you mean? You won't take it back?" I asked.

"When I found out Horace had taken a job in Texas, I also

noticed the other stations he'd interviewed with. I decided, 'Why not me?' The next day I emailed my resume to all the stations he'd turned down and got an offer. I'm going to tell Vick to shove it." He grabbed the handle of his car door and jerked it open. "Your wedding is my last gig here in Sugar Creek Gap."

"Wow. Good for you." I smiled, happy to see someone was getting what they'd deserved. "Tell my dad hello!" I called, waving him off, not sure if I'd really let him slide off the suspect list that easily.

I stood there at the top of the driveaway and waited for his car's taillights to disappear.

"What did he have to say?" Iris walked up behind me. She and I had already discussed how I thought Levi could've possibly had motive to kill Horace.

"I'm not sure Levi wouldn't be a suspect, but he did give me a good motive about the mistress." I sighed.

"Tracey?" Iris had a piqued interest. I nodded. "Melissa said," she started to say.

"Melissa also didn't tell us Horace took a new job in Texas or that they were working on their marriage." I nodded down the driveway. Levi's car was now out of sight. "Tracey and Horace didn't have any idea Levi Horn had heard so many things while he was cleaning. Tracey and Horace had planned to run off after Sandra died. I don't think Horace tried to kill Sandra, but I do think Tracey had enough motive."

"Where on earth were they going to run off to?" Iris asked.

"I'm not sure, but Tracey could've killed Horace out of passion." Buster interrupted our conversation as he bolted out the front door of the farmhouse, barking his head off at the sight of a rabbit hopping near the old barn.

Julia stood at the open door with Clara on her hip.

"Are you coming to open your presents or not?" Julia

moved her attention to Clara, who was clapping and babbling something with a joyful look on her face.

"That's not important right now. Let's go see what all everyone got me." I tucked my hand into Iris's elbow, and we strolled back to the house.

I was excited about opening gifts, and I was also excited to explore the new information Levi had given me.

Another suspect seemed to be woven into Horace LeLand's web of lies. Tracey Damski was next on my list.

Chapter 13

"That was a very nice shower." Mom sat in the passenger seat of my car. After I'd talked to Levi, I suggested that I drive Mom back to the diner, since it was on my way, and if I did that, my dad wouldn't have to leave the restaurant to come pick her up.

Originally, I'd planned to hang out at the farm for a little bit and play with Clara or even just help Julia clean up. When Clara had fallen asleep and all the other ladies had cleaned up for Julia, my head started to formulate even more plans about how I could get in front of Vick to ask him all the questions concerning the scandal within WSCG.

Not that he'd tell me, and I wouldn't really know unless I did ask him. It was the only way to find out real answers I needed about the affair. Melissa said she didn't care about the affair and really played it off—and she played it off well, if I had to add, because she fooled me. The more I thought about her laid-back attitude the louder it got in my head.

"What kind of woman doesn't care if her husband is having an affair?" I asked Mom on the way back to town.

"You're talking about Melissa and Horace, aren't you?"

She twisted slightly to the left in the passenger seat to look at me.

Rowena had found a nice comfy place in Mom's lap and took full advantage of the opportunity for some scratches. Buster was behind me, his head hung out the backseat window, trying to bite at the air with his ears pinned back by the wind.

Every once in a while, something would grab his attention, and he'd jerk his head to look behind the car or even let out a little yelp.

"I guess we never know what goes on behind closed doors." Mom sighed. "But I heard at the Elks from her own mom how Melissa and Horace had a strange marriage. Did you know Sandra loaned them all of her money? Every single penny."

"Yes, and that's what makes me think Tracey Damski might've killed Horace." I was crossing enemy territory with Mom, and I knew it, but I really needed to sort everything out in order to get a clearer mental picture.

"Was she the one who Horace had the ongoing affair with?" Mom asked.

"Yes. I wonder if she got caught up in the fame. When I heard from Lucy that Vick had cut everyone's hours and airtime, not to mention the funding for the Friday-night football broadcasts, I thought Levi might've had a good motive to kill Horace because he literally got the worst deal from Horace coming here."

"Your daddy and I miss those Sunday broadcasts. But the football games?" Mom's features hardened. "He has no business whatsoever in doing something like that. It's a sin not to have the games broadcasted on the radio. They did it when I was in school, when you were in school, and when Grady was in school, and I certainly want it to continue for Clara."

"We've got a long time until she gets there." I couldn't even begin to imagine Clara as a teenager in high school. The thought made my soul heavy with sadness. "Let's just keep her this age."

"Fine by me. With the way this town is changing, I'm not sure what we are going to do." Mom made it sound like she and my dad had talked about this.

"Hopefully, we can get this murder solved, and I plan on talking to Vick about some things." I gripped the wheel and kept my eyes on the old curvy road.

Dusk had started to move in. The sun's last bit of ray was barely visible between the trees that lined each side of the road. It was a good time of the night for nocturnal critters to start appearing, and there were no crosswalks for them, which meant I had to keep my eye on the road, even if I couldn't get my brain to cooperate.

"We? Don't tell me you've..." She stopped. Her eyes raked over me with a scowl. "You put this family in danger, and you'll have more than Horace LeLand's murderer to deal with."

"Don't be going and getting all upset. I'm not going to put anyone in danger. But if it helps Angela to collect clues, then it won't hurt. Besides, I really do believe Vince was now mistaken for Sandra when someone stabbed him with the letter opener."

"Like I told you and your dad earlier, I just can't help but to think we need to live in our apartment until all the crime is resolved." She huffed. "Do you think we need a new sheriff?"

"Angela is doing the best with what she's got. All these murders aren't because someone is out to just kill anyone. They've all seemed to be because of some sort of revenge. In this case, Levi had motive to kill Horace because his income was cut, among other reasons, but I do think that's the biggest. But then I think he didn't do it, because he took a new job that sounds like it's much better than the one he has here."

"That's a shame." Mom tsked.

"Though Melissa claims she has an alibi, I do think she'd have the best motive to have killed Horace. After all, he is benefitting from her mom's money even if Sandra isn't gone yet." I didn't want to say "deceased" because it just seemed awful to even think the word or put the idea out into the world. "And if he was planning on divorcing her, then he'd get half of the money."

"When Sandra told us about the little loophole their lawyer had found with Medicare, I wondered if it was legal. Your dad checked into it, and apparently, it sure is. Got us to thinking if we need to do that with you." Mom caught me off guard.

"Whoa!" I didn't even want to think of the possibility that they would need full-time care and move from their condo to the actual care center. To even think of them in that shape really was painful to imagine. "We don't need to put that on my plate right now."

"Someday you're going to have to come to the realization your dad and I won't be around." Mom brought to light my greatest fears of living without them.

"Luckily, you're in great shape and health, even though you eat all that gluten," I teased, trying to move away from this particular conversation.

"Ain't that awful. But I'm glad to see Julia and Grady take their doctor's advice. For now." She smiled. "Did you see Clara ask me for some nacky?"

"She's a doll." A satisfied sigh met the grin on my face. The sheer mention of Clara's name sent me into love overload.

"And to think Sandra doesn't know the joys of having a grandchild." Mom talked as though she'd gotten to know Sandra pretty well and considered her a friend.

"Why is Sandra in the main building at the senior living facility?" I wondered, though I had never asked anyone until now. "I guess she's okay, since Vince and she are kinda an item."

"You know about that?" She looked shocked.

The carriage lights of the downtown area were twinkling off into the distance as we got closer and closer.

"Not from him," I said sarcastically. "I saw them today at Pie in the Face, and they actually looked happy."

"She is." Mom's face lit up. "It delights me to even hear her talk about him. When he got hurt, it was painful for her not to see him. To answer your question, she said she didn't want a big place to clean. Though it's more expensive to live over there with the extra staff and all, and she doesn't require the care, she loves not eating alone."

"Wonder if she and Vince will move in together?" It would be so fun for Vince to find a true companion for the rest of his life. He deserved it.

"I think she's worried too much about Melissa now to even think about Vince. At least that's what I heard at the Elks." Mom was looking out the window as we passed the post office and then the old mill.

The mountains surrounding Sugar Creek Gap were now a silhouette from the darkness as it started to lie across our small town.

The sound of the old mill's wheel rumbling along with the trickle of the water as it pushed over the old wooden paddles was so soothing.

The old mill wheel was the first one built in our town when it was founded, and the preservation committee made sure to keep it running. Though we didn't have any mill operations today, the wheel was still a neat piece of history, and placing it right smack-dab in the middle of downtown made it a cool, unique feature.

I made a quick U-turn at the corner of Main Street and Short so I could park in front of the Wallflower Diner. Lights were on at the radio station, and I pictured Vick in there, mulling over what on earth he was going to do now that Levi had quit.

"Are you coming in?" Mom asked, apparently not sure whether she should pick Rowena up.

"Nah. I think I better get these kids home." I glanced in the backseat at Buster. He'd lain down.

Mom picked up Rowena and started to hand her to me so she could get out, and Ro wouldn't attempt to escape.

"Is that Vick?" I noticed him walking out of the diner. I pushed Rowena back into Mom's hands. "Stay here for a minute with the kids. I need to talk to Vick."

"Bernadette." Mom used her scolding-mom voice.

"It'll be a minute." I unclicked my seatbelt. "Roll down your window and listen so you can tell the ladies at the Elks'." I winked and jumped out. "Vick! Vick," I called to him just as he was walking past Mac's business.

"Good evening, Bernie," he said to me. "I was just talking to your dad about your big day. I guess congratulations is in order."

"Thank you." I offered a smile.

"Let me know what I can get you for a gift. I'm sure you two have everything." He was right about that.

"That's kind, and we really don't need anything. If you really wanted to do something, we are asking folks to donate to the Sugar Creek Gap High School Boosters. And from what I understand, you aren't going to broadcast the football games anymore."

My words struck him. He tucked his thumbs in the loops of his belt and rocked back just enough for me to see he was uncomfortable talking about it.

"I have a solution. I know hiring Horace really put a dent into the budget." I was gauging his response to see if I could even bring up Horace and the scandals he was embroiled in at the station under Vick's nose.

"Yeah. I'm always open to solutions." He indeed seemed to be open, so I continued.

"I went to see Kenneth at the golf course, and he is open to donating the funds needed for the football game broadcast, but there's one catch." I knew it was a hail Mary for us to be able to keep Levi here, but it was worth a shot. "Levi has to be the announcer."

"This all sounds really good, and I would've run with it an hour or so ago, but Levi has quit the station. Took another job out of town." Vick's jaw tensed. "It looks like Horace has taken more than himself to death—he's taken my station."

"What if we came up with a solution?" I had no real solution, but after I got some information about the scandal, I could at least try to come up with ideas.

"I'm listening." His eyes narrowed in crinkled slits. "Go on."

"First, we need to make sure listeners get the real scoop on Horace's murder."

He started to fidget and looked a little uncomfortable.

"I know it's hard to even think about," I continued, "but the station's reputation is at stake. You are losing listeners, not gaining them, because you wanted to win some sort of crazy award by bringing Horace here."

The exact opposite of what Vick wanted for WSCG happened once Horace came.

"From what I understand, there's been a big scandal there. From the cuts to budget, cuts to salaries, and cuts to all the programs with live airtime, it's all due to Horace's employment. Not only have your numbers dropped because your plan didn't give listeners any programs to listen to, but the affair between Tracey and Horace has taken a toll on everyone there." He went from surprised to taken aback, based on the way his face contorted with all the information I spewed at him.

"I understand you didn't think the public knew what was going on behind those glass windows down there, but we do.

We are a small town, and we loved listening to Lucy's Sunday-morning show. And Levi's live weather reports, even when they were way off base, but it was the small-town feel we all loved. Not the major broadcast Horace was going for. So the first thing I think you need to do is go back to basics. Have another meeting with Levi and offer him his full job back with a bonus to do the football games. The golf course giving their name and advertising dollars for that time alone should make up the salary Levi is getting to leave. Plus, he gets to stay here where he belongs."

I waited to see what he thought.

He gave a little nod, his jaw softened, and he sucked in a deep breath.

"I guess I could, but it'll have to wait until tomorrow. I'm exhausted and really just want to go home." He at least agreed to try, and that was enough for me.

For now.

"Can I ask you one more question?" I really had to get this information.

"Sure," he said.

"Can you tell me a little bit about the scandal with Horace and Tracey?" I could tell it was something he didn't want to discuss. "I really want to help get this dark cloud from lingering over the station while you go back to rebranding to the new way. That means bringing the scandal to light and possibly seeing if Tracey…" Instead of saying it, I dragged my finger along my throat.

"It's something I have always been against, and I should've stopped it the first day I found out about it. Not that it matters now." The disappointment covered his face. He frowned. "I've always taken pride in the station. It was doing well with ratings, but as a businessman, you should always be looking for ways to grow. I heard Horace was looking to make a move, and I took everything and gambled it on him. I didn't realize he was such a diva and that no one would benefit from him. The opposite happened. Everyone lost. With that came cuts, and I believed with time and higher rankings, the advertisers would come, and I'd be able to make up incomes, begin pay increases and bonuses again. The only one who benefited was Tracey. That is until Horace broke it off with her a little while back."

Now we were cooking.

"Tracey marched in my office and demanded I fire him for sexual harassment." My ears perked. "She said he hit on her and took advantage of her working alongside him, and if I didn't fire him, then she'd make sure the station went under. Now with Horace gone, he sure did leave a mess that I don't think can be recovered."

"So Tracey got what she wanted?" I asked. He shot me a confused look. "Revenge. You didn't want to fire him, and well, someone got rid of him putting a stain on the station."

"Bernie, are you saying you think Tracey killed Horace?" His eyes popped open at even the slightest inkling of this theory. His mouth dropped open, and his eyes fluttered as he looked down at the ground, trying to make sense of it all. "I guess she could've. She did say she'd make sure—but kill him?" He asked the question like it was never a possibility.

"Woman scorned. Horace had made her believe she was the cat's meow, and from what I understand, Horace had taken a new job and was leaving WSCG once his contract allowed." Vick had not been privy to that information. The shock rolled over him like a freight train.

"He what?" he snarled.

"Levi told me he'd found out about the new job he took because Horace had turned it down because he took a job in Texas." I started to feel a little bad for Vick. His obliviousness to what was happening at his station made it seem like he wasn't the great businessman he believed he was.

"He made a fool out of me." His jaw clenched. "Too bad

he's dead. I don't get the satisfaction of firing the dirty son of a b—"

He started to rattle off an expletive, but Mom interrupted him.

"Honey! I think the kids want to go home now." She'd gotten out of the car and indicated that she was tired of waiting for me and having to stay inside.

"I'll be sure to talk to Levi tomorrow when I get into the office, and I'll also call Kenneth. I think I owe him an apology too." Vick at least seemed to have listened to my theory and grasped that he'd started to divide our community away from his station.

"Don't worry. We will get WSCG back in the ranks and all the townspeople's good graces before too long. And bringing back the football games is your first step," I assured him before I let him go.

"Well?" Mom asked. "What happened?"

"I think we have our radio station back to how we like it." I pinched a smile and thought of how I had to make a point to stop in to talk to Tracey before she disappeared, taking what little secrets she might be keeping with her.

Chapter 14

Rowena and Buster had taken their spots on the couch after I fed them, rubbed on them, and let them do their nightly business, leaving me alone in the darkness of the night on the back patio.

Despite the excitement of Clara's birthday party tomorrow night, I still couldn't stop thinking about Horace's murder. After everything I'd learned about him, none of it was a good reason to kill him.

It must've been sometime after one in the morning when I dozed off in the chair. Buster's scratching the screen door, his way of asking to come out with me, woke me up.

"My goodness." I blinked a few times, trying to figure out why I was still outside, and jumped out of the chair. "What time is it?" I dragged myself out of the chair, thinking it was around two a.m. Boy, was I surprised when I went into the house and saw it was already five in the morning.

During the fall and winter, the mornings were dark outside, convincing me the clock in the kitchen was wrong. I picked up my phone and tapped the screen to bring it to life.

"Geesh, Bernadette," I groaned, knowing I would pay for

this later today when I'd be dragging from exhaustion. "You only have yourself to blame," I sighed, flipping on the coffee pot.

Shortly after, I checked on Buster to see if he was ready to come back in then filled his bowl and Rowena's up with kibble. In my bedroom, Rowena barely picked her head up off the pillow, not giving two cares in the world I'd not joined her there last night.

"I wish I were more like you," I told her, thinking of her lack of care for anything but food and a few scratches here and there. "Food and love. No other cares," I mumbled as I grabbed my robe.

I had barely enough time to take a hot shower and put some makeup on to hide the dark circles. Bags under my eyes not so much. Those would have to take a lot of cold compresses, and that couldn't happen this morning.

"Do you want to come with me?" As I was at the door about to leave, I saw Rowena had gotten under my foot.

Meow, meow. She nudged my leg with the top of her head before she brushed up against me, curling her tail around my shin.

"All righty. Let's go." I picked up the empty mailbag from the floor and tossed it on my shoulder. "You have to stay on your leash," I warned her.

The basket next to the door was where I kept all fur-baby things. Buster's sweaters, Rowena's leash, and their toys. Not that Rowena played with toys much. Buster was her toy, and she loved to bat at him a few times a day.

"You don't feel like taking care of Buster today?" She stood still for me to clip the harness and leash on her. Most cats would never let their human do that, but since I'd had her, I'd trained her to go on a leash when we needed to. "You're too precious." I clipped the leash.

She couldn't resist a few little nips at it before she purred and stood at the door.

"Buster." The sound of his name started his bolt toward the door. "You be a good boy, and maybe I'll exchange you two between my second and third loop."

He sat down looking at me with those big, sad brown eyes.

"You're a good boy." I didn't look at him when I closed the door behind Rowena and me, fearing I'd give in by making her stay there or trying to wrangle both of them on my route. The latter had proved to be impossible the last time I'd tried it.

People on the street were amazed when they saw Rowena, a cat, on a leash. Naturally, they'd run up to us and want to talk about it. Buster would not have any of that. He'd butt right on in and up to the people, wanting his fair share of attention. Then Rowena would swipe him because he got too close or he'd step on her. That would lead to a fight, and all you-know-what would break loose.

I've never brought them both again.

Rowena was the smartest cat ever. I was sure everyone thought their cat was equally smart, but she knew exactly the route to take. Once we were over the bridge and next to the veterinarian's office, she tugged the leash as far away from the building as she could.

"Don't worry." I laughed and reached down to pat her when she stopped on the curb so we could make sure no cars were coming. We had to cross Main Street to get to the post office. "I'm not taking you to the vet."

The garbage truck hummed by, sending Rowena behind me, giving a little tug of the leash.

"It's okay." I snatched her up so she didn't stay scared. "I'll never let anyone hurt you."

I snuggled her close to me and darted across the street, where I found Monica was busy checking the LLVs with the other mail carriers in the back parking lot. She didn't notice

Rowena and me go into the sorting room, where my first loop was already stacked and ready to go.

It was too dark for her even to see I had Rowena or she'd have stopped me. Monica, like everyone else in Sugar Creek Gap, loved the feisty feline, and if I was going to get some answers about Horace and Tracey's relationship today, I needed all the everyones to pat on Rowena so I could start conversations and see what new information I could pull out of people.

"My oh my, you brought the baby." Vince grinned when he looked down and felt Rowena rubbing up against him.

"Oh no. She's left a lot of glitter behind." I referred to the fur she'd left behind on his pant leg.

"I'll take her glitter any day." He scratched under her chin. "Isn't that right?" She took full advantage of Vince sitting on the swing and jumped up in his lap, not caring one bit that she needed to share it with today's newspaper. "What do you know?"

"I know that you have been dating someone and sure didn't tell me about it." I couldn't let him off the hook about Sandra.

"I wouldn't call it dating." He snorted and continued to rub on Ro. "We enjoy each other's company, and she loves to play Scrabble. Beats sitting alone every night."

"You still didn't let on about nothing." I wasn't giving him a pass that easily.

"Outside of the last few months of you making sure I was doing my physical therapy and what I needed to do to get back here, I would see you one time a day, maybe two if it was bingo night." He was making the point that we really only talked at this time every morning and not much more than that. "You've got a life. You've got your own parents to worry about. Not this old man."

"You know that's not true. Granted, life gets a little busy with Clara and my job, but I'm not too busy to come see you.

You've never asked more than a handful of times. And I've come each time invited." I reminded him that friendships were two-way deals. "But I'm not here to argue."

I had strapped my bag around me like a crossbody. I dug down to search for his mail. Monica usually put it on top. Rowena jumped down from his lap and chased a little bug on the concrete porch, causing her leash to extend all the way out, so I had to look through the mailbag with one hand.

"I guess you don't have anything today." I frowned.

"Good. No bills from the rehabilitation center yet." He brushed the fur off his lap. "I can't even begin to imagine what I have to pay out of pocket."

"Let's hope nothing. Medicare." Just saying the word reminded me of the loan Sandra had given Horace and Melissa. "Speaking of which…" I eased down on the swing next to him and looked out over the mountains, which made a beautiful backdrop.

It was like a picture. The sun was beginning to show life. Swirls of orange and yellow mixed in the clouds, giving a little hint of the green, red, and orange leaves woven from the branches of a tree like a well-stitched quilt.

"Do you think Tracey Damski has enough motive to have killed Horace?" I truly wanted to know where Vince stood on this theory. "I hesitate to even ask. I'm worried you aren't able to look at this objectively."

"I don't let anyone or anything, not even a little companionship, come into play when I need to solve a case. Though I'm retired, someone still tried to kill me." He lifted his finger and jabbed his chest. "We don't even know if the two crimes are tied, but the circumstances led to it, so when I tell you that all emotions of my friendship with Sandra are put aside when you and I discuss the particulars, I mean it."

"Fine." I put my hands in the air with no other choice than to believe him unless he proved me wrong. "I talked to Levi yesterday, and he told me he'd caught Horace and Tracey at the office every Sunday night to have their little affair."

"Makes sense." Vince nodded up and down. "Sandra and Melissa always have Sunday supper together. Kinda like you and your family."

I smiled at the thought. It was something my mom had started when I was born. She made sure we went to church every Sunday. She'd come home from service and spend all day cooking homemade, mouthwatering food that we'd devour at suppertime. Dad had to come in from working the farm, and I had to come in from playing outside.

The tradition continued through the years, and now Julia hosted Sunday supper for everyone, but I did the cooking. Vince and Iris participated most of the time.

"That's why you've not been to the farm those few Sundays before your accident."

"Stop calling it an accident. It was an attempt on my life." He was insistent.

"You know what I mean. But I think it's nice that Sandra and Melissa do that." I smiled, thinking of Vince having his own little family, one that Sandra had seemed to pull him into. "Levi's hours had been cut."

Vince interrupted me, "Yep. Read that in the paper." He picked up the newspaper and showed me the front page. "Tells all about it right here. Said an anonymous source distributed all the information."

"Anonymous?" That was certainly interesting. I leaned over to get a look at the paper.

"They report the source sent it from one of the emails from the station. A general email."

"Do you think it was Sandra or Melissa?" I had to ask him. "Possibly went in to clean his office out?" I knew the theory was far-fetched, but I had to leave no stone unturned.

"Why would they know the insider information?" He made

an excellent point. "Besides, it does nothing for either of them to bring the radio's scandals to life. It does say something in here about Horace having an affair, though it doesn't name Tracey specifically. Melissa wouldn't ever want that to come out now."

"Lucy Drake?" I questioned.

"Now, Bernie. Think about it." He scolded me like he hadn't taught me a thing about investigating. "Do you think Lucy Drake would accuse Horace of having an affair with someone there and let people think she could be the mistress?"

"You're right. She's definitely worried about her reputation." Lucy made sure she was always presentable and very professional. She'd never do anything to ruin her gig. She loved being a DJ, but she also loved that morning show. I continued, "Yeah, but if she can point fingers at someone else so she's not one of Angela's suspects and get her show back, she might throw something out there."

"People do lose their moral compasses when they are desperate. What are you going to do about it?" His brows lifted.

"We are going to deliver the mail as usual, and I might try to pop in to talk to Vick and Lucy if they are there." It sounded like a plan was coming together. "One problem, I can't spend too much time on this today. I've got to get all my deliveries made before Clara's birthday party." I got up. Rowena went from sitting to standing. "Are you coming?"

"Sandra and me." He couldn't contain his smile as her name crossed his lips. It was pretty sweet to see this new emotion he was wearing.

"Great. Do y'all need a ride?" I asked. Instinctively, he took Rowena's leash, since she couldn't go in. Some of the residents were allergic to her glitter. When she came with me, Vince and Rowena were able to spend some alone time together.

"No. I actually called Grady and asked if Melissa could

drop us off. He said of course and even invited her, but I've yet to ask." Rowena rubbed all around Vince's legs. He put his hand out.

"Just one." I opened my mailbag and took out the few cat treats I'd thrown in there. "I'll be right back."

The place was silent and empty when I went in. For this reason, I delivered there first. I enjoyed the quiet. It was a nice way to get work finished and start the day.

My phone buzzed a text from Grady. Instead of calling, he said he was running late. He and Julia had stayed up late to decorate for the party, and he was late getting home from football practice. Something about someone getting injured, but he didn't name who. I was guessing it was someone on the second string.

"Are you ready?" I found Rowena curled up in Vince's lap, a sure sign her belly was full of treats. He'd folded the paper up to make it easier for him to do the crossword puzzle.

"She's pretty comfortable." He handed me the leash. "She's a good girl."

Rowena jumped out of his lap and got a spurt of energy as she darted toward a fly.

"I'll see you tonight unless I hear anything about the," I put my hand up to my mouth, shielding it like I was telling a secret. I whispered, "Murder."

I left him laughing. We both must have felt pretty joyful, even though it didn't look like I would solve the murder before any of the festivities.

While picking up my second loop of mail from the post office, Monica already had a line of customers, so Rowena didn't get to see her, even though Ro had tried to go down the hall where the counter was located.

I had to be careful when she was with me because of the people who had allergies. I certainly wouldn't want to hurt anyone.

Today was one of those days when every shop was busy, so a quick in and out with Rowena tucked in my bag as I exchanged the incoming mail for any outgoing mail was a good switch of pace.

Another thing I noticed was the absence of chatter about the murder. The speakers along the sidewalk on Main Street were pumping out Lucy Drake's morning show, making me think I could possibly get some face time with her or even see if Vick was there.

Rowena continued to bat at little bugs along the way. I kept her on my left side so she wasn't near the street just in case she decided to dart when a car drove by. There was no way I was going to take the risk.

She and I stood outside of Pie in the Face, looking into the bakery window. Iris was behind the counter, and a few employees were busy with customers. When she noticed me, I waved and pointed down at Rowena.

A huge smile grew on her face, and immediately she grabbed something that wasn't outgoing mail. We waited for her to come outside to get her mail.

"There's the baby." She had some homemade cat treats in her hand. Rowena stood up on her hind legs and gave a couple of meows that led into a loud purr. "Aunt Iris loves you," Iris said to Ro in a baby voice while giving her the treats.

She stood up and ran her hands down the front of her apron. The wind whipped up as a car drove past. Rowena leapt in the air to snag a piece of paper floating from the street.

I picked it and put it in my mailbag, even though I knew the street sweep would be by shortly. It was part of the garbage service. The garbage truck came through and got all the garbage picked up. Then the street sweep vehicle would follow up, grabbing all the pieces of trash that fell out of the garbage truck.

The service was part of the money the Beautification

Committee had gotten from a grant they'd received from an award for the town's entry into one of the many Kentucky Coziest Small Town contests.

"What's the word?" She wanted to know if I'd heard anything about Horace.

"I saw the paper, and no one has even mentioned it on my route, and I can't go into the diner, since I have Rowena, so I'm going to rely on you to get the 411." That was my way of telling her to get the information.

"I read the article, too, and whoever is chicken poo to do it anonymously?" Iris rolled her eyes. "I have a feeling it's someone who knows way more than they are telling."

"Yeah. They are anonymous." I shrugged.

"What if it's the killer?" Iris asked.

"Why would the killer do such a thing?" I wasn't following what she was saying.

"They are pointing fingers at the affair, making it look like the affair or the unnamed mistress had motive." She'd started down a whole different trail of sleuthing.

"And that's why if Angela reads the article, she'll explore that path, giving the killer some more time to figure out how they aren't going to get caught." I bit my lip. "I have to go. I need to see Lucy or Vick."

After I left her standing on the sidewalk, Iris hollered, "I'll see you at the party!"

At the rest of the shops on Main Street, I was able to slip the mail in the mail slots with Rowena stuck down in my bag so she didn't leave a trail of fur behind her.

"There's my grand-cat." Mom had met me outside to grab her mail after I'd texted her I had Rowena. She didn't need to get the mail, since it was junk today. "Do you think I was going to let you pass by without giving her a little bit of granny love?"

Mom had taken a piece of boiled chicken and given it to Ro.

"She's going to go home ten pounds heavier if I don't drop her off at home." My reason for taking Rowena was to see if I could hear something, and a little bit of exercise wasn't going to hurt either. "Did Vick come in this morning?"

"He didn't. I'm guessing he's trying to smooth things over from the newspaper article. His ship is burning down." She frowned. "I imagine he'll lose his job over all this."

"Why do you say that?" I knew the obvious, but had she heard something.

"Today when Lucy came in, she had the paper under her arm. I asked her about it, and she told me the big dogs were coming into town to have a meeting." Mom shimmied a shiver as a cloud passed over the sun, bringing with it a cool breeze. "'Heads are going to roll' were her exact words."

"Do you have any biscuits and gravy to go?" I knew that dish was one of Vick's favorites, and I could use it as an excuse to see him.

"I sure do." Mom gave me a theatrical wink and disappeared into the diner.

Rowena was getting fidgety and probably needed to go potty, which was her way of telling me I was on limited time.

Shortly Mom emerged and kissed me goodbye with two to-go boxes of biscuits and gravy. One was for Mac.

He was on the phone when I went into Tabor Architects, but it didn't stop him from walking out of the office and giving me a kiss in exchange for the biscuits and his mail. He gave Rowena a few pats too. She purred happily and enjoyed spreading her fur around as she moved from item to item.

"I'll call you in a minute," he whispered before turning his attention back to the call.

Grady had written in his text that Julia had stayed home today to finish decorating for Clara's party, so I knew I wouldn't be seeing her at the office.

Lucy Drake was sitting in the DJ box with her headphones on. An advertisement was running on the air.

I peeked into the glass window to get her attention.

She looked up, dragged the headset off her ears, and hit a button before she came outside.

"Is Vick in there?" I asked when she walked out. "Mom said he didn't come in the diner, so she sent this with me for him."

"Yeah. He's a nervous Nelly in there." She gave a little grin and rubbed her arms as if warding off a chill. "Did you see the paper?"

"Yes. Who do you think sent it in?" I asked.

"I have no idea, but Vick is on the rampage to find out. He's called the station lawyer and even the newspaper. He said everyone is making him look bad." She snorted. "Really, I think he's worried about his job because he was the one who took the chance and made the decision to hire Horace. Even when we all came to him about the budget he cut. We knew this was going to be the death of the station."

"Are you worried about your job?" I asked.

"I'm worried they might shut us down because he'd paid Horace all the money and blew the budget until next year. But he did tell me about you getting Kenneth to agree to sponsor the football game broadcasts. That's a step in the right direction." She jerked her head to look in the glass window when someone appeared.

That someone was Vick.

He wildly gestured her to get back in the DJ seat. His brows formed a *V*, but they softened when he saw Rowena and me.

"I've got to go. He said we all had to be on our top game today when the big dogs get here." She turned to go back in. "Thank goodness there's not an airport close by and they have to drive here. It'll give us some time to group."

Vick was still watching us, and I held up the to-go container. He lifted a finger for me to wait, and he and Lucy passed at the door.

"Mom sent this over. She notices when her favorite customers don't come in for their food." I tried to smile to assure him everything was going to be okay and that he had a community standing behind WSCG. "I'm sorry you're going through all this."

"My ego got in the way. And I've pretty much singlehand-edly killed the station. Should've been me stabbing Horace and not some wacko." In no uncertain terms, he was about talking the demise of his career as though he could see it coming.

"Maybe Sheriff Hafley will get it solved, and you can save the station if you truly think it's going to shut down." I knew it was highly unlikely for her to solve it in what few hours were left before the station meeting. "Have you thought about a plan for them to give you some time to see if you can breathe the station back into a good financial standing?"

"I've got a lot of ideas, but my staff is so mad now that I've cut their bonuses, incomes, and on-air time I'm not sure they're even staying. They are all either dropping like flies or flying off." He took the biscuits and gravy. "Thanks again for talking to Kenneth. I asked Levi to do the broadcast, but he didn't commit. He still says he's leaving."

"Don't lose hope. Let the big station owners see what they have up their sleeves. Maybe they can extend the budget and save something. I know Lucy isn't going anywhere. Any chance you can get her show back and running?" I wanted to help with any and all suggestions I could.

"It's part of a proposal with stats I'm going to present to them. She's playing hardball, though. Demanding things I can't give her." He didn't say what things. "I can't help but wonder if she wrote that article in the paper."

"Do you think the affair could be the reason for the murder?" I asked.

"I don't know?" Vick's eyes grew. Apparently, he wasn't privy to the gossip swirling around the station and what I knew as a fact from Melissa. "Geez." Vick ran a hand through his hair. "She's got to be the one who killed him."

"I wouldn't go in there pointing any fingers, but check all her computer files and see if anything was sent from her computer." It was a good suggestion and a sure way to see if she'd sent it.

"I will. Just another thing to put on the list. You have no idea how it feels to constantly be looking over my shoulder to see if anyone is going to come after me with a letter opener," he murmured under his voice as a couple of people walked past us on the sidewalk.

"I can only imagine how nerve-racking it is." I frowned. "But if you can find anything out and tell Sheriff Hafley, the sooner the better. I guess time is of the essence before the meeting."

"You're right. I am going to go in there right now and talk to Tracey." His jaw clenched. "I hate this for Melissa."

I didn't tell him how Melissa knew about the affair. It wasn't my place to tell, and she wasn't a suspect in Angela's investigation, so I didn't need to cast a doubt in Vick's mind when I needed him to look within his station to see if the killer really was in there.

Chapter 15

"Happy birthday to you."

The crowd had gathered around Clara. She was sitting in her high chair underneath the big tree in the farmhouse's backyard, a pink party hat on her head. The cone-shaped hat had a huge fuzzy ball on the top and pink feathers around the bottom. She looked like a little princess.

There were at least twenty Mylar balloons in various shades of pink tied to the back of her high chair along with a big numeral one for the year.

She clapped in delight while everyone sang her name in the birthday song. Julia didn't put a candle in the pie Iris had made, and Clara didn't wait for everyone to stop singing before she dug right on into the gluten-free apple pie.

Julia had told Iris to bring the pies instead of making different ones, and no one knew any different. Any pie baked by Iris was delicious whether it was gluten free, sugar free, or fully loaded. She had never made a bad pie.

Grady and Mac were standing off from the crowd, each holding a plate of pie with a scoop of vanilla ice cream on top.

When I approached, my mouth watered at the sight of the pools of cold ice cream around the warm pie.

"Are you sure I can't get you a piece, Mom?" Grady offered.

"No. I already didn't stay on schedule for walking my route to help lose a little weight. I surely don't need to gain it in the next forty-eight hours." I patted my backside, referencing how I wouldn't look so good in the pantsuit I'd picked out for the wedding.

"You're going to be a beautiful bride." Grady was so sweet.

"We still have the big game to get through." I knew he and Mac would much rather talk about football than a wedding.

"We were just discussing some of the injured players." I could hear the worry in Grady's voice.

Being part of the coaching staff, let alone the coach, of a highly popular sport didn't come without a price or a worry, especially when the town expected you to bring about a winning season.

It wouldn't take but one or two big losses for the school board to get some heat from the community to get a new coach. This was one rare occasion when being part of a community all of your life was overlooked, and the good of the team took precedence.

I wasn't proud of it, but I'd been part of that mindset when Grady was in school. When he became the coach, I'd totally changed my mind.

"Are they on the first string?" I asked.

"A couple linebackers, and if we don't hold the line, we just might see." Grady's voice broke. He couldn't bring himself to say loss." "We will see. That's all we can do."

"We will be fine. I've been working with the line on some of the plays they run." Mac was talking about plays from the opponent. "If they study the tapes I compiled tonight and tomorrow at run-through before the game, we should hold steady."

The chat turned to more technical plays and positions when I saw Clara starting to nod off in her high chair. It was a good opportunity to go over and help Julia.

"Saved by the mawmaw." Julia hugged me. "What would I do without you?"

"I think it's the other way around." Julia handed Clara to me. Clara was covered from head to toe in sticky apple pie. "You'd think she'd be hopped up on sugar."

"She's had a sugar crash." Julia and I laughed as we watched Clara bobble her little head then jerk and try to open her eyes.

"I'll take her in and get her cleaned up," I told Julia. She placed her hand on her heart as a gesture of gratitude.

The farm looked so pretty. The party lights we'd strung around for the wedding were a great little touch for the princess party.

When I passed clusters of guests, they all put a hand on Clara.

"She's a doll, Bernie." I stopped for a second so Melissa, Sandra, and Vince could get a glance at the now-sleeping one-year-old.

"I think so too, but I'm biased." I winked and headed inside the farmhouse to see if getting her cleaned up would wake her up enough to try to open one of the many presents the guests had brought.

No such luck. I'd taken her back to her bedroom, where I laid her in her crib and got some pajamas for her. When I undressed her, she was as limp as a rag doll.

I used a baby wipe instead of a warm washcloth to clean her up. She was sleeping so well, I didn't have the heart to wipe her completely down.

The chatter of the party caught my attention. I walked

over to Clara's window and peeled back the sheer curtain to look out with gratitude at all the folks who had gathered to celebrate her.

Many faces I recognized from football games, but I didn't know all of them. There were teachers from the school and various members of the staff. Some of Grady and Julia's college friends had also come in for the event. They were still all very close, and I loved when they went to visit them and let me keep Clara for the weekend.

It was special Mawmaw and Clara time. Mac was so respectful of that time too. Just seeing all the friends supporting Julia and Grady warmed my heart.

I moved my eyes to the Front Porch Ladies. Julia was sweet to have thought about making a little outdoor fire with some chairs around it for them. She knew they'd get cold, and she didn't want to leave them out of the fun.

All four of them seemed to be enjoying themselves while they ate their plates of ice cream and pie.

I forced myself to look away.

"There you are," Iris whispered from Clara's bedroom door. "I was wondering if you escaped." She walked in holding her plate of deliciousness.

She came up behind me and placed a hand on either side of my shoulders.

"Whatcha looking at?" she asked, stuffing a spoonful of pie in her mouth.

"All the love out there." I smiled and lifted a hand across my body to pat her hand. "You're a very good friend, in case I've not told you that in a while."

"Yes I am," she joked. "And you're going to really think that after what I just heard."

"Yeah, what?" I curled up on my toes and glanced in the crib to make sure we weren't waking Clara.

"You aren't going to believe what happened today while

you were on your third loop." Iris kept her voice low. "The Wallflower Diner had run out of pie, and I was taking some down there when I noticed Angela Hafley's sheriff's car was parked outside of the radio station."

Iris had my full attention.

"Apparently the article in the paper—the anonymous article," she clearly stated, as if I didn't know what she was talking about. "Angela felt like some answers to Horace's murder were still in the station, so she gave Vick a warrant to take all the computers, everything that even ran WSCG as evidence to see who might've sent the article from the station's email server."

"Poor Vick," I sighed, feeling deep sadness for him.

"No joke. The big station guys were already there. Angela didn't care. She forced them all to leave while the deputies cleared out everything."

"Everything?" I asked, knowing there had to be some other sort of tip Angela had gotten for her to go to this extreme.

"Mm-hmmm. Even the employee files from their own desks. That was when they discovered all of Horace's files were gone. Missing. But she had enough sense to go looking for a paper shredder." Iris was making exaggerated hand gestures. "All the files had been shredded. They found the empty file sleeves on top of the shredder. So they know someone knew it was garbage day and shredded all the files."

"Oh no." I remembered seeing the garbage truck this morning.

"'Oh no' is right. Angela sent some deputies out to the dump site to find the garbage from the station. She insists they will put together the shredded files to solve Horace's murder."

I couldn't believe what she was telling me.

"What about Vick?" I had to know the details.

"He was beside himself. Not because of the files but the bigwigs can't run the station with no computers, so they said the employees had to go to the Lexington station to keep

WSCG on remotely. And they had to go today. This afternoon." Iris's words hit me in the gut.

"Wait. Are you saying all the employees had to go to Lexington—as in they're already in Lexington?" I asked, a quiver in my throat.

"Yes. So I hate to say it, but the big game probably won't be broadcasted." Her comment was the least of my worries at this point. "What's with the panicked look on your face?"

"Levi. Did Levi go?"

"I said everyone. Well, everyone but Tracey Damski. They can't find her." Iris smiled but didn't realize why I was asking about Levi.

"Back up." I knew I needed to revisit the topic of Tracey's absence, but I also had to make sure Levi was gone. "Levi went?"

"I said yes." She raised her voice.

We both jerked over to see if Iris woke up Clara. She was still zonked out.

"Why?" Iris took another bite of her pie.

"What's a wedding without a DJ?" I asked. The words hit her as the color drained from her face.

"Oh, Bernie. I do think he left with them." The lines between her eyes creased as she realized what I was getting at.

I sucked in a deep breath as the reality of the situation started to wash over me.

"I can't think about that right now. Tell me about Tracey." I had to try to stop myself from a nervous breakdown. We were at T-minus 36 hours until my wedding day, and here I stood at the wedding venue without a DJ?

"There's not been any sight of her. The deputy on the police scanner said she wasn't home. Angela clicked back and told him to go in because she had a warrant." The story Iris told me was sounding more and more like a thriller movie than a real-life Sugar Creek Gap saga. I eased down in the rocking chair, snuggling the stuffed cat to my chest. My eyes glazed over Iris's piece of pie.

The more I tried to look away, I just couldn't.

"The deputy went into the house, and there didn't seem like anything was missing. I guess they really don't know what she had, but her toothbrush was there, and so was some meat in the refrigerator." Iris took another bite of her pie.

"All of those things tell me she'd not been planning to leave," I said. "Which makes me think she didn't leave on her own." I stood up and put the stuffed animal back in the rocker. "No Levi, no Tracey." I gripped the edge of Iris's plate.

"What are you doing?" Iris tugged back on it.

"Taking this." I tugged a little more, and she released it. "We need to find Tracey, and we need to find a different DJ."

"I have a record player." Iris tried to make light of the situation just as a crack of thunder exploded in the sky.

"Great." I stuffed a big spoonful in my mouth, not caring a bit if I had to pour myself into my pantsuit for my big day. This little bit of stress relief was much needed.

Chapter 16

Every time my phone beeped throughout the night, I jumped to see if it was Levi. I'd left him at least five—well, twenty voicemails and possibly fifteen text messages.

"Listen, I understand you don't want to tell me you can't DJ the wedding, but I'd appreciate it if you'd just text me. You don't even have to call me to confirm." I left him another message and hung up the phone.

My eyes just wouldn't close, and Buster knew it. He flipped and flopped next to me in the bed, popping his head up and seeing me staring back at him. Rowena had not a worry in the world. She was curled up on the pillow next to me, her paw resting over her eyes.

"She's going to have to give up that pillow soon. That's just between you and me," I told Buster. He took it as a sign to army crawl his way up to my face and give me a few licks.

I gave up and decided to get out of bed. I slipped my feet into my slippers and grabbed my robe on the way out of the bedroom.

"Leave it to me not to be able to sleep in on my day off. The day before my wedding," I groaned and complained to Buster, who had gotten out of bed with me.

The expanding feeling in my chest at the uncertainty of what Levi was up to was almost too much for me to bear.

"It's Bernadette Butler." As hard as I tried not to text Levi—"just one more time," I told myself—I did it anyway. Heck, I had nothing better to do but wait for Buster to come back from going outside for a potty break. "I'm not sure why you'd even go to Lexington, since you're leaving WSCG," I said, using the speech-to-text feature and leaning up against the back door.

I reread over it and started to hit the back button but instead hit Send.

"I'll pay you triple if you just come back or even call me. Honestly, I'm at a crossroads here. If you don't come, I might just have to dance to a record player from Iris Peabody." I continued to text and send my thoughts to Levi.

"Stop, Bernie." I dropped the phone in the pocket of my robe. "Wait." I took it back out and hit Levi's name under the text app. "Just let me know you're okay. From what I understand, Tracey is on the run, and I sure hope you've not been stabbed. Apparently, she's the sheriff's number-one suspect."

That was my final text to him.

For now.

"Hi, Lucy. Iris told me about what went down at the station yesterday. I hate to ask for a favor, since I know you're in Lexington, but can you please tell Levi to call me or at least ask him if he's planning on coming back to DJ my wedding tomorrow?" I hit Send and then followed up with, "I will save you a piece of cake for when you get back. I hope and pray everything works out and they catch Tracey!" I sent a few fist-pump emojis to finish out how I felt about what was going on.

Buster was taking his sweet time. Normally, if he needed to go out in the middle of the night, I would be rushing him back inside so I could go back to bed. Not this time. I was wide awake, and I would be more anxious trying to force myself to sleep instead of just fixing my coffee and staying up.

Then I decided it was time to pull out my notebook and use what pent-up anxiety I had on laying out the facts of Horace LeLand's murder while I waited for the coffee to brew.

My phone rang. Excitement jumped within me.

"Levi?" I pleaded out loud and picked up the phone. "Hi, Iris." I rubbed the back of my neck. My heart felt like it was shrinking back into place. "What on earth are you doing calling me at this hour?"

"What are you doing texting me at this hour?" she questioned back.

"Oh my goodness." I pulled my phone from my ear and hit the message app. I noticed I'd messaged Iris, not Lucy. "I'm sorry. I meant to send it to Lucy. Did I wake you?"

"Yes, but more importantly, happy wedding eve!" she yelled just as the sound of rain started to hit the roof of my little house.

I got up from the table and opened the screen door. Buster couldn't stand the rain, and it would not be too much longer until he bolted to the door.

"I'm sorry I woke you," I said. Buster darted in. I held the door and looked out into the dark sky to see if I could see any stars. "No stars." I let go of a heavy sigh. "There doesn't seem to be anything going too great for tomorrow."

"Like you said, one great event out of three isn't bad." She was talking about what I said while she and I were in Clara's bedroom.

"If it had to be one of the three, that was the most important one." I grabbed a mug on my way over to the coffeepot. It smelled so good, and I couldn't wait to take my first drink. Carefully, I carried it over to the table. Buster looked between his bowl and me, very confused. "Buster thinks it's time to eat. Poor guy."

I sat down in the kitchen chair and laid the phone on the table then hit the speaker button so I could be lazy and not hold the phone to my ear.

"I'm up now. I'm coming over. You don't sound good to me." Iris didn't need to use her intuitive instinct to hear the worry in my voice.

"I'm good. I've just waited for tomorrow or just the happily ever after only for it to not just rain but to have to dance to your record player," I half joked.

"Did you make coffee?" she asked.

"I'm having a hot cup now." I put both hands around the mug and enjoyed the first savory sip.

"I'll bring the coffee cake." She clicked off before I could protest, which would've been half-hearted because I wanted her to come over.

Buster had taken himself back to bed, where Ro still hadn't moved. I grabbed the notebook, my mug, and a blanket to take outside. I decided I would sit under the cover portion of the patio and listen to the soothing rain. I'd wished for the wet stuff to go away, but if I had to be honest, I truly loved the sound of the ticking rain on the roof and welcomed the calming of my nerves.

I'd also text Lucy again.

The shrill sound of the metal gate opening rang above the rumbling thunder in the distance.

"Hey, Iris. Back here," I called into the darkness so I didn't scare her when she did see me.

"Girl. What on earth are you doing out here?" She still had on her pajamas with a raincoat over them. The cake pan was in her hands. "Don't you see we are having a horrible thunderstorm?"

"According to the time between clap of thunder and the lightning, we have about ten minutes until it reaches us." All the wives' tales my mom had told me when I was growing up had stuck in my mind. If there weren't stars in the night sky, the next day was going to be rainy. Or the time between a clap of thunder and a lightning bolt was how far away a storm was. Neither had ever failed me.

"Besides, it's soothing to me right now." I looked up at her.

"Get inside," she ordered and led the way. "Come on." She held the door until I was going to listen to her.

She worked around the kitchen to get a knife, a spatula, and a couple of paper towels, and she put a big piece of coffee cake on the towels and set it in front of me.

"You need a refill." She grabbed my mug and filled it up, and then she came back and joined me. "So, why aren't you sleeping?"

"I've been busy texting and calling Levi. I venture to say if he was on the fence about DJ'ing the wedding, he's totally off the fence. Not even on a rung." I picked at the crumb top before I took a piece and put it in my mouth. "I'm sure I've proved to him I've lost my mind."

Iris put her hand out for my phone, and I slapped it into her hands. There were zero secrets between us, and that included our passwords. We'd made a pact before I started to date Mac that we needed to know each other's passwords in case either of us died. We had only each other, and right now, she was the only person I wanted to be with.

"So who cares about a DJ?" After she'd read the texts I'd sent Levi, she shrugged and put the phone down. "We don't need music. Though I did try to see if my record player worked. Sadly, the speaker is a little crackly."

I laughed. Just the sheer thought of us changing records at my wedding put a smile on my face.

"See?" She pointed with satisfaction. "I got you to smile. Just think, you and Mac are finally going to be husband and wife just like it should've been all those years. But," she said, quick to follow up before I butted in, "we are grateful it wasn't, because we want to thank Richard for giving us Grady, which led to Julia and now Clara."

"You are such a good friend. You always know how to make me feel so much better." I looked at her across the table, and I swore the wrinkles on our faces told me we'd gotten older, but when I looked into her eyes, it felt like we were sixteen and sitting on her bed.

"From the sounds of the recorded weather report I heard on the way over here, it sounds like these storms are going to be here all day." When she lowered her voice at the end of her sentence, I knew she was hinting that the football game might be cancelled.

"Then I hope Mother Nature gets it out of her system before tomorrow." I held up my mug, and so did she. Both of us did an air toast with them before we lost our minds in a round of giggles.

Ro jumped up on the table.

"Look who decided to join us," Iris teased

"She's not one to miss a good time." I reached over and patted the feline.

"What's with the notebook?" Iris asked.

"Since I was awake, I thought I would just jot down some clues."

Iris's head tilted, and her brow rose.

"I know. They have Tracey to find, or maybe they found her, but why would she go to the trouble of shredding the files? That doesn't even make sense. The emails and possible correspondence with Horace through the computer I can buy, but the files?"

"I had the scanner on all night, and nothing came over, so I'm assuming they've not found her yet." Iris and I sat in silence as we ate our coffee cake and sipped our coffee.

Knowing her as well as I did, I could tell she, too, was

thinking about the murder, the facts we'd collected, and what she'd overheard.

She broke our concentration when she took her phone and hit the screen.

"I'm going to call in sick today. I've gotten all the orders done. Your wedding cakes are completely ready for tomorrow. No way." She wagged a finger at me when I started to protest. "I won't take no for an answer. We are going to have a day in. We are going to order Uber Eats and sit in there while watching murder mysteries. It'll be fun and relaxing, and we just might get a few tips or ideas about Horace's killer."

It didn't take much for me to give in. A rainy day, huddled underneath the covers with Rowena and Buster while my best friend was with me sounded like something a good psychiatrist would tell me to do.

And it was what we did until I got a call back from Lucy around five o'clock. Yes. Everyone who loved me called me to ask about the big day tomorrow and if they needed to do anything. Mac had sent me flowers from Leaf and Petal, which would brighten any bride's day. And with a quick phone call to let me know the game was cancelled because of lightning, Grady and Julia also wanted to make sure I was set.

They all told me they were praying for the rain to clear, and deep in my heart, I knew if it didn't, then the wedding Mac and I would have was the one that was meant to be. Instead of letting anyone know the deep sorrow in my heart over the loss of a perfect day, I already knew I'd won the lottery when it came to family, friends, and a wonderful and loving community.

Even Vince sent a couple of texts to make sure I was all ready, and I was. As the day ticked away with each movie Iris and I watched, the more excited I got.

Until…

My phone rang, and it was Lucy.

Chapter 17

"I'm so sorry it's taken me this long to get back to you. You aren't going to believe the events unfolding here." Lucy's voice contained a mix of excitement and nervousness. "To answer your request for me to ask Levi, he never showed. He's, like, missing or something. Kinda like Tracey, but I bet he didn't come because why would he? He told the higher-ups he'd taken a job elsewhere, but I have to say they came back with a cushy offer that I don't see why he'd turn it down. They gave him until tomorrow to think it over. So he's not here."

"You mean to tell me he's been in Sugar Creek Gap all this time?" That annoyed me. I'd been trying to reach him a few hundred times. I spent the day checking my phone in case I didn't hear a text ring in—and for what? Nothing! "If he tries to call me, I'm not taking it. So what else is going on there?"

"They fired Vick. Something about some sort of important paper in the mail, but Vick swears he never got it. Of course, we know how responsible you are, and you always deliver the mail. I told them and recalled to Vick how you were at the station, and he came out when he saw us talking." She rambled on as my memory did an awful thing.

"Oh no." I jumped up from the couch and ran over to the door, where I'd dropped what I thought was an empty mail bag. I opened it, turned it upside down, and gave it a hard shake. Two items dropped out. A piece of certified mail to WSCG, which was what Lucy had to be talking about, and the piece of paper Rowena had batted from the street that'd floated out of the garbage truck. "Lucy." I tried to stop her from talking.

"They offered me the job!" she squealed. "You are talking to the new station manager of WSCG!" I pulled the phone from my ear and cringed.

"Lucy, Lucy…" I continued to call her name until she realized what I was doing.

"What? You don't sound happy, Bernadette. I know your wedding is tomorrow, and I'm sorry about the weather forecast, but can't you be a teeny-tiny bit happy for me?" she asked me, but little did she know I was holding the piece of mail that got Vick fired.

"I'm so happy for you." I didn't really know what to do. There was no sense in me telling her, but I could tell Vick. "Is Vick there now?"

Iris had gotten up and picked up the second piece of paper, which Rowena had taken a vested interest in again and batted around. Iris wagged it in front of Ro as they played a little bit of cat and Iris, a version of cat and mouse.

"Oh no. He hightailed it out of here once they axed him." Her voice held such glee that I started to feel sick to my stomach. But I knew what I had to do.

After a few more congratulations between us both and a confirmation she'd not heard from Tracey, we finally got off the phone.

"I have to go see Vick Morris." I showed her the certified mail. "I completely forgot to deliver it with the stack of mail yesterday, and I think this is a reason he got fired."

"He got fired?" Iris's shock and a big gulp showed in her emotions. She dropped the piece of paper on the floor, and Rowen pounced on it, kicking her back feet to try to cover it up. "Over mail?"

"I guess it looks pretty important." I frowned. "I have to take it to him. If I'm the reason he got fired, let's just say I have to make it right."

"Only if we can stop and pick up some chicken from Kentucky Fried." Iris drove a hard bargain, but I was all in.

"Deal." I picked up the mailbag and the piece of paper Rowena had now left behind and tossed both the certified letter and the scrap paper in the bag. "Do you want a pair of sweats to put on?" My eyes shifted up and down Iris, who was still wearing her PJs, since she'd not left my side today.

"Nope. I'll just crawl in bed with you tonight, and tomorrow I'll go home and be fresh as a daisy for the wedding." She dangled her keys in the air. "I'm driving."

"You two be good." I looked back at Ro and Buster. Buster looked defeated that I wasn't taking him, but Rowena was too busy licking her paw to clean behind her ears to care.

In usual Iris style, she put on the music we loved to listen to in the eighties on the SiriusXM stereo in her SUV, which doubled as her Pie in the Face delivery vehicle. She sang to the high heavens along with Cyndi Lauper's "Time After Time."

My toe tapped all the way to the neighborhood where I did my third loop. Vick's house was one of the first houses built in the neighborhood when he took his job at WSCG. That was a long time ago, when Richard was alive.

Iris turned down the radio.

"You can't possibly beat yourself up over this. If he got fired over one piece of mail, then they were searching for something to fire him over, like the lack of judgement in hiring a meteorologist for a market where we can simply look out our doors to know a storm is here." She snorted and zoomed past the country club before making a right into the subdivision. "Heck, even Horace got the weather wrong three-fourths of the time."

"I know. Nothing makes sense about the whole thing." I looked off into the distance. "I was actually thinking about him when Richard and I had come to see Vick's house after a football game one night."

"I don't remember y'all doing that." Iris was always so gentle when reminders of my past life crept into our conversations.

"We did, and Vick was so proud of it. He said he was going to finish his career off in that house. It was Richard yammering on and on how we needed to move to the city, the new neighborhood so Grady would have friends next door, and that led into a huge fight. He blamed me for wanting to live at the farm, and I blamed him for not being grateful it was free. It all snowballed."

"Which one is his?" she asked once we'd gotten past a few houses on the main drag.

"Take a right back on Runny Meade Court, and he's the house dead in the center of the cul-de-sac." It was the best lot in the neighborhood, in my opinion.

It was a two-story brick with a back wooded lot that, if you weaved your way in and out of the trees, would put you at the fifteenth hole of the golf course.

"Man, I wonder what his mortgage is per month." Iris pulled up in the driveway, leaned way over the wheel, and looked up. "This has to be about six thousand square feet."

"I'd say it's a little bigger than that." I grabbed the mailbag from the floorboard and shook out the letter. "You stay here. I'll be right back after I do a little song and dance to at least make him feel somewhat better."

"Offer him the first dance tomorrow, since you won't have to do it because there's no DJ." Iris made a joke that I didn't find too funny. "I'll wait here. Maybe clean up some of the trash." She did have a lot of things, like cake spatula wrappers, invoices, empty cake boxes, and items she might need on the road.

"Why on earth do you keep that big metal spatula in here?" I shook my head and got out of the car.

"You never know when it'll come in handy." She reached behind her and picked it up off the back seat. "We might need it tomorrow for your wedding, and I'll have it handy. Besides, I don't tell you how to deliver the mail." She picked up the empty bag and gave it a little toss back to the floorboard.

The thought of Iris delivering the mail sent a giggle through me that I had to force myself to stop when I stepped up on Vick's front porch and rang his doorbell.

"Bernie, what are you doing here?" His voice came through the security camera tied to his doorbell. "Don't you have a wedding to get ready for?"

I leaned in and looked into the little blue light, figuring that was where I was supposed to look.

"I had some last-minute mail pieces to deliver." I held up the certified piece of mail.

"You can leave it at the door. I just got out of the shower." His reply gave me a yucky mental image.

"I have to get a signature. It's a certified piece of mail." I held the yellow part where he needed to sign up to the camera.

"Okay. I'll be down in a minute," he said, leaving me there for more than a minute.

I stepped off the porch a couple of times and looked back at Iris's car, but she was pulled up too far, and I could see only the back bumper. When I heard loud footsteps coming from inside the house, I put a smile on my face and wondered what on earth I was going to say if he asked.

"Hi there," he said. "Where's a pen?"

"Oh." I realized I probably should've brought one. "I don't have one. Do you?"

"Yeah." He let out a sigh like I was putting him out. "Come on in."

"Do you remember when Richard and I came to see your house before it was finished all those years ago?" It was neat to see how it turned out, even though it was a little dated now. I followed him into the two-story kitchen, which had three skylight windows in the ceiling.

"I forgot all about that time." He rummaged through a kitchen drawer. "Richard really liked it. I remember he came back the next day and asked me how much it cost, if there were any lots for sale."

"He did?" I watched a few more dark clouds glide by the skylights through the beating rain. What sounded like a clap of thunder rumbled the ceiling. "I don't remember Richard telling me that."

"I don't think he was going to." He slammed the drawer shut and opened another one. "He said there was no way you would leave the farm, but he would in a heartbeat."

"He was right for as long as Grady was home." I didn't want to hear any more about Richard. "I thought you were in the shower." I noticed his hair wasn't wet when I took a closer look and saw the dirt on his hands. Clearly, he wasn't taking a shower when I rang the doorbell.

"I have to run upstairs to get an ink pen." He looked so put out and didn't even register my statement. "I'll be right back."

"I'll be here." I tapped my fingernail on the kitchen counter, twisted around to look around at how Vick had decorated his house, and concluded I honestly didn't know much about the man other than what I learned from daily mail exchanges.

The thud I'd heard before happened again, only this time it sounded like it was coming from the room and not thundering from outside. Curiosity was one of my biggest vices, and I certainly wasn't very proud of it, but I had to know what type of dog he had in the room that wanted out. At least it sounded like a dog. Whatever was in there was whining and thumping around.

"What are you doing?" Vick asked. I'd not heard him come back from upstairs. He had an ink pen in his hand.

I took my hand off the doorknob of the door where I'd heard the noise coming from.

"I think your dog wants out." I turned the handle and opened the door to find Tracey and Levi tied up back to back, both with gags in their mouths.

They were both trying to say something at the same time.

Their eyes grew and were looking past me. I quickly turned around in time to see Vick rushing toward me but not before Iris appeared behind him and ran after him with that darn metal spatula in her hands. She gave him one good whack on the head, knocking him flat to the ground.

"I told you it was going to come in handy." She twirled it around in the air like she was some ninja as the sound of sirens echoed in the background.

Epilogue

To say the wedding was amazingly beautiful was an understatement. Mother Nature had given me the gift of a gorgeously bright, sunny, and crisp fall day with no rain in sight. Clara looked adorable sitting next to Rowena in the little wagon. Buster walked next to Julia, pulling that wagon, as she walked down the pathway to the altar before Grady walked me down to greet Mac.

The flowers looked even more delightful than the photo Sara had showed me at the Elks Club. After Grady shook Mac's hand, I turned around, and all eyes were on me. My parents were in the front row. Vince, Sandra and Melissa sat behind them. All my co-workers filled in the seats, and even Monica was crying tears of happiness.

Iris recited a beautiful poem about finding the perfect love, not leaving a dry eye on the farm. Even Levi did a fantastic job spinning the tunes up until midnight. By that time, all the guests had left full of good homemade food and delicious Pie in the Face cake.

Not once did anyone mention what had taken place at Vick's the night before. No talk of how he'd confessed to stabbing Vince, thinking he was Sandra, in hopes Melissa would force Horace to leave Sugar Creek Gap, and Vick could bring the radio station back to what it was before Horace had come there.

When Horace had figured out Vick was behind the stabbing, he'd sent Vick the emails telling him that he'd contacted the big station owners about how Vick ran things, hoping Vick would lose his job. Horace wanted to make that his penance for trying to kill Sandra. It was obvious by the email Vick had written back to Horace, which Rowena had found. Just by chance, that email had made it into my mail carrier bag then the floorboard of Iris's dirty car. I'd thought it was just a piece of trash that'd fallen out of the garbage truck that morning, but Rowena knew. It wasn't until I was inside Vick's house and Iris really did start picking up trash that she actually read what was on the torn piece of paper. While I was inside, she knew there had to be a problem and put two and two together. Luckily for me, her metal spatula did come in handy. Just not at my wedding like she'd suggested before I got out of her car. Iris was smart enough to have called Angela before she barged into Vick's, freeing Tracey, Levi, and me.

After the last piece of cake was put away, and we'd helped Grady and Julia clean up, they decided to give us their gift.

"Bbbb," Clara babbled when Grady asked her to tell Mawmaw something. The little one had not fallen asleep all night. "Bbbb."

Julia mouthed along with Clara, giving a couple slow nods as if she were encouraging Clara to say what she was supposed to say.

"Baaaby." Clara clapped.

"That's right." Julia stuck a positive pregnancy test in front of Mac and me.

My jaw dropped, and my eyes grew big as the news of Julia's pregnancy settled on me.

"When did you find out?" I stood in the old farmhouse kitchen with my husband by my side. Tears flooded out of my eyes and down my face.

Grady proudly held Clara in one arm and wrapped the other around Julia, both with bright smiles on their faces.

"Last night I was feeling a little sick, and I didn't think there was any way, but I took the only test I had in the house, and when it turned up positive, I about died." Julia looked at Grady.

"She made me take her and Clara out in the rain to go to the hospital and get a blood test to confirm." He squeezed his family closer to him. "I knew there was a reason for that storm, and I'm grateful the game was canceled."

The five of us stood in the small farmhouse kitchen hugging one another, overcome with joy and filled with happiness that would last us a lifetime.

Iris's Coffee Cake

1 stick butter softened
  3/4 cup sugar
  1 tsp vanilla
  1 egg
  2 cups flour
  2 tsp baking powder
  pinch salt
  3/4 cup milk
  Filling
  3 tablespoons butter softened
  1 tablespoon cinnamon
  1/2 cup flour
  1/2 cup packed brown sugar
  Topping
  5 tablespoon butter softened
  3/4 cup flour
  1/2 cup packed brown sugar
  1 tablespoon cinnamon

DIRECTIONS

1. Preheat the oven to 350F.
2. In the bowl of a mixer, cream together the butter and sugar, scraping down the sides occasionally. Add the vanilla and egg, mix in.
3. In a separate bowl, mix together the flour, baking powder and salt. Add one half of it to the mixer, and when mostly combined, add the milk. Once the milk is mostly incorporated, add the rest of the flour.
4. To make filling: in a small bowl, pinch together the softened butter, flour, sugar and cinnamon until soft crumbs form.
5. To make topping: add the butter, flour, brown sugar and cinnamon to a food processor and pulse until coarse crumbs form (You can cut in with forks or a pastry cutter, but I am not patient enough for that!).
6. Grease a 9x9 baking pan. Pour in ½ of cake batter, and spread to all four corners. Sprinkle the filling over top, then pour in remaining cake batter, and spread carefully across the top, disturbing the filling layer as little as possible (an offset spatula works well for this).
7. Sprinkle the topping over the top and press lightly so it adheres.
8. Bake in preheated oven for 45-50 minutes, until a toothpick inserted comes out clean. Cool to warm on a wire rack before serving the coffee Cake

Pumpkin Sugar Cookies

Ingredients
   1/2 cup pumpkin puree
   1 egg yolk
   2 tsp vanilla
   14 Tbs room temp butter about 1 3/4 sticks
   1/4 tsp pumpkin pie spice
   1 tsp cinnamon
   1/2 tsp salt
   1/2 tsp baking powder
   1 1/2 cups sugar
   2 1/2 cups all purpose flour OR equal amounts of gluten
free flour
   5 drops yellow food coloring optional
   3 drops red food coloring optional

DIRECTIONS:

1. In a large mixing bowl, combine room temperature
   butter and sugar with a mixer

2. Slowly incorporate the egg yolk, pumpkin puree, vanilla and food coloring
3. In a separate bowl, combine flour, baking powder, salt, pumpkin pie spice and cinnamon
4. Gradually mix the flour mixture into the pumpkin mixture and combine well
5. Refrigerate dough for 30 minutes
6. Preheat oven to 350 F and spray cookie sheet with non-stick cooking spray
7. Using your hands, roll dough into small 1-inch balls and lightly roll them around in a bowl of sugar to coat
8. Evenly space dough balls apart from each other on cookie sheet and gently press down with a fork or spatula
9. Bake for 10-12 minutes
10. Allow to cool briefly on pan, then place on cooling rack to prevent the bottom from over cooking on baking sheet

Enjoy!

A NOTE FROM TONYA

Thank y'all so much for this amazing journey we've been on with all the fun cozy mystery adventures! We've had so much fun and I can't wait to bring you a lot more of them. When I set out to write about them, I pulled from my experiences from camping, having a camper, and fond memories of camping.

Readers ask me if there's a real place like those in my books. Sadly, no. It's a combination of places I've stayed and would own if I could.

XOXO ~ Tonya

www.Tonyakappes.com

For a full reading order of Tonya Kappes's Novels, visit www.tonyakappes.com

FACEBOOK
INSTAGRAM

GOODREADS

Join like-minded readers like YOU in the Cozy Krew Facebook Group for dream casting, fan theories, and live Q & A's. It's like a BIG GIANT BOOK CLUB! But if you want to have your own book club, be sure you let me know! I love to send goodies.

Also By Tonya Kappes

A Camper and Criminals Cozy Mystery
BEACHES, BUNGALOWS, & BURGLARIES
DESERTS, DRIVERS, & DERELICTS
FORESTS, FISHING, & FORGERY
CHRISTMAS, CRIMINALS, & CAMPERS
MOTORHOMES, MAPS, & MURDER
CANYONS, CARAVANS, & CADAVERS
HITCHES, HIDEOUTS, & HOMICIDE
ASSAILANTS, ASPHALT, & ALIBIS
VALLEYS, VEHICLES & VICTIMS
SUNSETS, SABBATICAL, & SCANDAL
TENTS, TRAILS, & TURMOIL
KICKBACKS, KAYAKS, & KIDNAPPING
GEAR, GRILLS, & GUNS
EGGNOG, EXTORTION, & EVERGREENS
ROPES, RIDDLES, & ROBBERIES
PADDLERS, PROMISES, & POISON
INSECTS, IVY, & INVESTIGATIONS
OUTDOORS, OARS, & OATHS
WILDLIFE, WARRANTS, & WEAPONS
BLOSSOMS, BARBEQUE, & BLACKMAIL
LANTERNS, LAKES, & LARCENY
JACKETS, JACK-O-LANTERN, & JUSTICE
SANTA, SUNRISES, & SUSPICIONS
VISTAS, VICES, & VALENTINES
ADVENTURE, ABDUCTION, & ARREST
RANGERS, RV'S, & REVENGE
CAMPFIRES, COURAGE, & CONVICTS
TRAPPING, TURKEYS, & THANKSGIVING
GIFTS, GLAMPING, & GLOCKS

Kenni Lowry Mystery Series
FIXIN' TO DIE
SOUTHERN FRIED
AX TO GRIND
SIX FEET UNDER
DEAD AS A DOORNAIL
TANGLED UP IN TINSEL
DIGGIN' UP DIRT
BLOWIN' UP A MURDER

Killer Coffee Mystery Series
SCENE OF THE GRIND
MOCHA AND MURDER
FRESHLY GROUND MURDER
COLD BLOODED BREW
DECAFFEINATED SCANDAL
A KILLER LATTE
HOLIDAY ROAST MORTEM
DEAD TO THE LAST DROP
A CHARMING BLEND NOVELLA (CROSSOVER
WITH MAGICAL CURES MYSTERY)
FROTHY FOUL PLAY
SPOONFUL OF MURDER
BARISTA BUMP-OFF

Holiday Cozy Mystery
FOUR LEAF FELONY
MOTHER'S DAY MURDER
A HALLOWEEN HOMICIDE
CHOCOLATE BUNNY BETRAYAL
APRIL FOOL'S ALIBI
Father's Day MURDER
THANKSGIVING TREACHERY

Also By Tonya Kappes

SANTA CLAUSE SURPRISE
NEW YEAR NUISANCE

Mail Carrier Cozy Mystery
STAMPED OUT
ADDRESS FOR MURDER
ALL SHE WROTE
RETURN TO SENDER
FIRST CLASS KILLER
POST MORTEM
DEADLY DELIVERY
RED LETTER SLAY

Magical Cures Mystery Series
A CHARMING CRIME
A CHARMING CURE
A CHARMING POTION (novella)
A CHARMING WISH
A CHARMING SPELL
A CHARMING MAGIC
A CHARMING SECRET
A CHARMING CHRISTMAS (novella)
A CHARMING FATALITY
A CHARMING DEATH (novella)
A CHARMING GHOST
A CHARMING HEX
A CHARMING VOODOO
A CHARMING CORPSE
A CHARMING MISFORTUNE
A CHARMING BLEND (CROSSOVER WITH A
KILLER COFFEE COZY)
A CHARMING DECEPTION

A Southern Magical Bakery Cozy Mystery Serial
A SOUTHERN MAGICAL BAKERY

A Ghostly Southern Mystery Series
A GHOSTLY UNDERTAKING
A GHOSTLY GRAVE
A GHOSTLY DEMISE
A GHOSTLY MURDER
A GHOSTLY REUNION
A GHOSTLY MORTALITY
A GHOSTLY SECRET
A GHOSTLY SUSPECT

A Southern Cake Baker Series
(WRITTEN UNDER MAYEE BELL)
CAKE AND PUNISHMENT
BATTER OFF DEAD

Spies and Spells Mystery Series
SPIES AND SPELLS
BETTING OFF DEAD
GET WITCH or DIE TRYING

A Laurel London Mystery Series
CHECKERED CRIME
CHECKERED PAST
CHECKERED THIEF

A Divorced Diva Beading Mystery Series
A BEAD OF DOUBT SHORT STORY
STRUNG OUT TO DIE
CRIMPED TO DEATH

Also By Tonya Kappes

Olivia Davis Paranormal Mystery Series
SPLITSVILLE.COM
COLOR ME LOVE (novella)
COLOR ME A CRIME

About Tonya

Tonya has written over 100 novels, all of which have graced numerous bestseller lists, including the USA Today. *Best known for stories charged with emotion and humor and filled with flawed characters, her novels have garnered reader praise and glowing critical reviews. She lives with her husband and a very spoiled rescue cat named Ro. Tonya grew up in the small southern Kentucky town of Nicholasville. Now that her four boys are grown men, Tonya writes full-time in her camper she calls her SHAMPER (she-camper).*

Learn more about her be sure to check out her website tonyakappes.- com. Find her on Facebook, Twitter, BookBub, and Instagram

Sign up to receive her newsletter, where you'll get free books, exclusive bonus content, and news of her releases and sales.

If you liked this book, please take a few minutes to leave a review now! Authors (Tonya included) really appreciate this, and it helps draw more readers to books they might like. Thanks!

Cover artist: Mariah Sinclair: The Cover Vault

Made in the USA
Columbia, SC
26 September 2023